Otaro Maijo

Otaro Maijo

Translated by
Stephen Snyder

HAIKA SORU

SAN FRANCISCO

Original title: **Ashura Garu**
Copyright © Otaro Maijo, 2003
Originally published in Japan by Shinchosha Publishing Co. Ltd.
English translation Copyright © Stephen B. Snyder 2014
All rights reserved.

Cover and book design by Sam Elzway

This book has been selected by the Japanese Literature Publishing Project (JLPP),
an initiative of the Agency for Cultural Affairs of Japan.

HAIKASORU
Published by VIZ Media, LLC
1355 Market Street, Suite 200
San Francisco, CA 94103

www.haikasoru.com

Library of Congress Cataloging-in-Publication Data

Maijo, Otaro, 1973- author.
 [Ashura Garu]
 Asura Girl / Otaro Maijyo ; translated by Stephen Snyder.
   pages cm
  ISBN 978-1-4215-7537-7 (paperback)
 1. Serial murders--Fiction. 2. Suspense fiction. I. Snyder, Stephen, 1957-
translator.
 PL856.A46A8413 2014
 895.63'6--dc23
                        2014024941

Printed in the U.S.A.
First printing, November 2014

CONTENTS

Part One:
Armageddon

1

THEY TOLD ME it would be okay, so I went ahead and did it. But of course it got messed up. No way it *wasn't* going to get messed up—or lost completely. My self-respect.

Now I want it back.

That's what I want to tell him, but I know it won't help. Sano isn't about to give it back to me, and self-respect isn't something a person can give you back anyway. You've got to get it back yourself. It was a bad idea in the first place to do it with somebody I don't really like. For one thing, he didn't say he liked *me*—he wasn't even really a friend. We go to the same school, but we don't hang out with the same people, aren't in any classes or clubs together. So why did I do it with him?

Because I was drunk. That's what I'd like to say, but that wasn't really the reason. And it wasn't what you'd call an "ethical lapse" or anything fancy like that either. The truth is…I did it because I was curious.

The size of Akihiko Sano's penis was the punch line for a lot of jokes around school. Everybody said it was microscopic, and I guess part of me wanted to see if the rumors were true, just for the hell of it. Or maybe it was because I'd heard he knew some special "technique," something he did with his fingers to make up for his micro-dick. But the truth is I don't care about "technique." If I don't like a guy at least a little, I just can't get into it...But then again I did get wet with him, which I suppose had something to do with what he was doing, so I guess you could say the rumors were true—on both counts.

So there I was, letting Akihiko Sano do all this weird stuff to me...and somehow getting off on it.

Gross!

It makes me feel sick when I think about him, butt naked, scrambling around and pawing at me and muttering all that idiotic crap. "You like that?" "You like it there?" "How 'bout that?" "Say something!" "Tell me when you want me to stick it in. I'm ready!" "You're dripping. Listen! Hear that?"

No, I don't! Cut it out! I'm *not* saying a thing. I don't want you to "stick it in"—ever! No *thank* you! I'm not getting on top of you, I'm not sucking it, and the fact that I'm wet down there has *nothing* to do with you. You could get that sound out of an ear or a nostril or any other hole if you mashed it around that much!

Maybe because his dick was so small, it got annoyingly, weirdly hard. Creepy hard, and bent out of shape or something. And it was inside me!

Eww!

He was trying to do what he'd seen in porn videos. All that spinning around and yanking my arms and legs—it made me queasy.

And then he tried to come on my face!

Asshole asshole asshole asshole! With his filthy little disgusting prick. Asshole asshole asshole mega asshole!

You don't come on a classmate's face!

He nearly got me. I was pretty much zoned out, just hoping he was almost done, but luckily, when he started grunting I realized what kind of nasty trick he had in mind. In the nick of time. If I hadn't, he would have shot his filthy load all over my face—and my self-respect would have sunk down into some cold, dark, lonely hole where no one could ever find it again. It would have just faded away, been shredded to tiny bits.

But luckily my self-respect wasn't about to give in that easily, not in the face of Akihiko Sano's cum. Fortunately, I have great reflexes and I managed to twist out of the way at the last second, so his semen landed only on my arm.

Shit! What do I mean "only"? That junk on my precious left arm! From now on, when my mom calls me for dinner, I'd like to pop off that arm like a mannequin or Barbie Doll, hide it under my bed, and show up at the table with just my right. My arm has been polluted by that pervert. I need my arm for kendo and tennis!

Having managed to avoid the face shot, I wiped my arm with the sheet and looked around the room. There wasn't much chance of finding a bamboo sword or tennis racket in a love hotel, or anything else I could use as a weapon, so I did the only thing I could. I screamed at him. "What the *hell* do you think you're doing? You *asshole*!" And then, since he just sat there grinning, still holding his prick, I kicked him in the face.

He groaned and fell back off the bed. I had nothing more to say to him. Some black guy, like LL Cool J, was suddenly talking in my head, speaking English no less. "Okay all right, girl. So get the fuck out of here! Now!" he said, and he kind of clapped his hands or something. So I threw on my panties and bra and T-shirt and pulled on my skirt. Sano was sprawled on the floor, rubbing his face. "Ouch!" he giggled. "Wow! Is my nose bleeding?" I ignored him, grabbed my bag, opened the door, and was out of there.

But then it hit me. Shit. Money. For the room.

I could just leave the whole bill for him to pay. But I knew that was no good. I didn't want him coming after me for my half. I pulled three one thousand yen notes from my wallet, opened the door, and tossed them in. They fluttered to the floor near Sano's shoes.

"What?" he sputtered. "Hey, wait! Where are you going? Aiko! You can't do this!" But I could. I turned my back on his bare-assed self, his dinky prick, the whole disgusting scene, and closed the door. The last thing I saw was my three thousand yen, scattered there next to him like a cruel sacrifice. Then I ran. From his gross face shot. From his overrated "technique." From this stupid mess. From my stupid self.

Though the last was the hardest. No matter how much I tried.

Other girls must have done it with Sano before me, but when I started to consider what they could have liked about all that pawing and grunting, I realized I'd been had. The whole thing was a scam—a trap meant to end with the face shot that the others maybe hadn't managed to avoid.

I imagined how shocked they'd been. Which was probably why they'd never said a word about it, just told me he was good and I should give him a try if I had the chance. And I'd fallen for it like a complete idiot—Complete Idiot Number…?

So, then, will I shut up about the face shot too? And tell some other girl he's good, that she should give him a try if she has the chance? That his dick's really small but his technique's fantastic? No, I will not. It might be fun to imagine somebody annoying like Reiko or Shoko getting it in the face, but I'd never tell them they should do it with Sano. My self-respect may have taken a beating, but it wasn't that far gone.

Truth is I don't want anybody to know I did it with him. I'd rather forget it ever happened. Or better yet, if I could, I'd rather make it so it really *hadn't* ever happened.

But that fucker is going to talk tomorrow at school. So I guess I have to fight back, make him look like the idiot he is, tell everybody he tried to come on my face but I managed to dodge and give him a good kick for his trouble.

Or maybe I won't. Maybe I'll just let him make a fool of himself—anyway, no matter what I do the guys are going to imagine me starring in a face shot like the ones in their videos. I can't stand thinking about it. Can't stand *them* thinking about it. Sano naked, fucking with me. Back door, me on top. Shit.

Maybe I'll skip school tomorrow.

But then they'll think I have something to hide, and it'll only be worse. No, I'll go. I don't like running away from trouble... at least that's what I tell myself. But isn't that exactly what I was doing? Running away? Running. Running. That's how I ended up at a hotel having meaningless sex with Sano in the first place.

The real idiot...is me.

The world is full of losers, and lots of them probably end up sleeping with someone they don't like. And some of them probably get cum on their faces. My brother said more people rent adult movies than any other kind, so there are plenty of guys like Sano who learned everything they know about sex from porn; and if all of them are trying to come on some poor girl's face, there must be lots of victims out there. All those assholes trying to shoot their nasty jiz—pyu, pyu, pyu—right on your face. Totally tragic.

Of course, I came within inches of totally tragic myself. And in the end, what's the difference? No matter how much I pity myself, it doesn't do me any good. I made my bed, so to speak, and

I have to lie in it. Having other people pity me isn't going to save me, either. There's really no one out there who'd be interested in saving me anyway.

So I have to do it myself.

But how?

First step: stop pitying myself.

When my brother isn't spouting statistics on porn rentals, he's been known to say that self-pity is a total drag—you sit around feeling sorry for yourself and never get anywhere. "I can't stand narcissists, like Miki Imai," he says. "They go around saying how much they love themselves, but in the end they're only talking to themselves. Anybody who talks about himself all the time is a douchebag in my book." Of course, he's never even met Miki Imai, much less talked to her. But that's what he says. Anyway.

So I've decided to stop talking about myself so much.

Okay. So what to do instead?

First off, how about getting cleaned up? Get rid of this gross Sano filth. A bath! It's only fifteen minutes from Shinjuku to Chofu on the express, but it never seemed so long.

I finally made it home and took a shower. But somehow I still didn't feel clean, so I ran a hot bath and got in for a soak. As soon as I did, I remembered the bubble-bath ball I bought at the Body Shop, so I climbed out, wrapped myself up in a towel, and went upstairs to get it from my room. When I got back, I tossed it in the tub— and just about gagged on the stink: lavender. Usually, I can't stand bubble baths *or* lavender, but when I get depressed, there's nothing like something a little exotic…at least that's what I've decided lately as part of my "self-therapy." Pretend a bit. It seems to work. Today I'm Kerstin, one of my very favorite people. I'm a Swedish exchange student who has come to America for high school, and sometimes I get letters from my brother, Olle, who lives back in Sweden, out in the countryside. He asks me what it's like "there" (by which he means Boston) or tells me that "here" (a village called Hadetbra—that means "Farewell" in Swedish) he's busy with his sheep; that he's going to buy a ticket sometime soon and pay me a visit "there" so we can go see the crocodiles at the zoo. He's never seen a crocodile before…or so his letter says. Kerstin has come all the way from Sweden to live in America, but she's not the least bit scared or homesick. She has no hang-ups—the kind of girl who takes life in stride. Whether she's in tiny Hadetbra or big, bustling Boston, she keeps her perspective. She just gets it. She knows who she is and never gets bent out of shape. She might seem a little standoffish at first—but that's just because she's so awesomely cool, calm, and collected. She makes friends with all kinds of people, and she has lots of them—friends, that is, boys and girls. She seems so together that these friends naturally come to her for advice about their love lives. Of course, Kerstin sometimes admits to herself that she has worries in that department like anyone else; but she knows she'll have to solve them herself, and she still gives the most perfect advice to her friends. Giving advice is simple enough.

Kerstin has some simple advice for Aiko Katsura in Tokyo as well: Aiko, sweetheart, sleeping with people you don't like just makes you lonelier. Fake warmth from a body that means nothing only makes you colder. Fake "relations"—fake fucking!—leaves you farther from the world, not closer to it.

I get it. And I have to admit that it feels like there's a huge chasm, an insurmountable distance between me and the world right about now.

But, Aiko, you shouldn't worry so much about "distance." Pay attention to the "road," the "way." That's what's real and concrete; "distance" is just a vague concept.

"The 'road' is long, but the 'distance' is just a fleeting dream."
Is that it?

That's it, Aiko. If you spend your time thinking about how
far you've strayed from the world, you'll end up like Noguchi or
Hasumi, jumping off a bridge somewhere. Or, like the Round-
and-Round Devil, you'll go from flaying stray cats and dogs in the
neighborhood to chopping up those little boys—triplets not even
a year old—down by the river.

I'm not crazy.

Who said you were? And why would it matter? But the point
is…who do you really like?

What? Who do I like? Well, I guess the first name that pops
into my head is Sekiya.

Sekiya? That's just a reflex. You saw too much of him in middle
school.

But he was so cute back then.

So what? As soon as he got to high school, he quit kendo, joined
the tennis club, and started to party, party, party. He stopped going
to school and turned into a complete jerk. You didn't think much
of him then, did you? Totally disappointing. It's not him, Aiko. So
who do you really like?

River Phoenix?

I was under the impression he's slightly dead. And besides, you
don't know anything about him. You just like him because he went
out with that weird Martha Plimpton for a while.

No one knows anything about celebrities, really.

So forget celebrities. There must be somebody you like right
here in the real world.

Kasami?

You only went out with him for two months.

Ishiyama?

No dates, nothing but sex.

Nakagawa?

You were just flattered that he asked you out. Aiko! These guys are all history. I mean someone new, someone now. There must be somebody. Somebody you still like? Somebody you've always liked?

Sagara?

Sagara!

I think I really like him. Sometimes I suddenly want to see him so much I can hardly stand it.

But, Aiko, you put a question mark after his name just like all the others. When somebody asks you who you like, you don't answer the question with a question. Love has no room for doubt. It's absolutely sure of itself. You don't say, "I may perhaps like so-and-so." That's just wrong. This is about your one-and-only, your everything—it should be the clearest thing in the whole wide world.

So, Aiko, there must be someone you were interested in even before you started going out with Sekiya. Someone you wouldn't trade for Kasami or Ishiyama or Nakagawa or Sano.

That's so Kerstin.

And there is, of course. I know it's not right—though I'm not sure why, or who it would hurt to admit it. Me maybe? Anyway, I'm sorry, and I know it's too queer and boring and all that, but I can't help it: for more than six years now I've been in love with a boy I knew in elementary school. Yoji Kaneda. My first love, but I never seemed to get over him. What can I say?

I sighed and slipped deeper into the bath. The sigh blew away the bubbles, and I could see the murky water over my belly and legs. Had Sano really been touching me down there just a little while ago?

I started to get depressed again, but then Kerstin reappeared and said just the right thing: You can't let something like that get you down, Aiko. There are plenty of people out there who are ready to do bad things to you, even worse than Sano did just now.

That's right. Kerstin is amazing. She always knows just what to say. And she's absolutely right about this. It could have been worse. What if Sano had managed to hit me in the face? Or even worse than that, what if he had asked me to let him come in my mouth, had stuck his little dick in and forced me to swallow. Or—nooooo!!—even worse still, the worst would have been having him come inside me and getting me pregnant. Having Sano's baby inside me. I swear I would have killed him and raised the baby by myself. Inside the fence. In the cage. Like one of those girls in *Caged Fury*, fighting the other prisoners and guards tooth and nail to protect my child. But even with the baby and all, that would still be the worst. I don't want to go to prison…or even pretend I'm in *Caged Fury*, and I don't want to raise my baby behind bars.

So I guess I got off pretty easy. All kinds of people out there are ready to do all kinds of bad things to you.

And when I get to this point in my thinking, that poor man appears again, somewhere in the back of my brain. That black guy locked up in the basement by those weirdos, chained in the dark and fucked from behind by those two perverts. He's really strong, like LL Cool J. So when he gets free he shoots the balls off the pervert who's been fucking him, and then Bruce Willis asks him, "Are you okay?" and he says, "Nah, man. I'm pretty fucking far from okay." I'm pretty fucking far from okay. Which makes sense, since they'd stuck some weird ball in his mouth and were fucking him up the ass. I'm pretty fucking far from okay. I always feel so sorry for him.

But what about me?

Am I okay?

Not really.

But it could be worse. I managed to avoid a face shot, cum in my mouth, getting pregnant, and playing *Caged Fury*.

I'm okay.

I wouldn't call it the best day of my life—in fact, it totally sucked. But I'll live. I'll move on.

I suppose I'm not the only stupid girl who ever slept with a guy she didn't like. I bet there are more of them out there than I can imagine. And I bet a lot of them got cum on their faces or in their mouths, or even inside them and ended up in prison protecting their babies. Well, maybe not the *Caged Fury* part. But none of it matters anyway. What matters is that I got into a stupid mess, but it wasn't the worst mess possible.

I'll learn from my mistake, and I won't ever sleep with somebody I don't like ever again. Really. And I'll find someone new to fall in love with. Someone different.

Who am I kidding? There won't be anyone new, and I'll be so lonely I'll sleep with the first guy who comes along…only, this time I won't. I really have learned my lesson…though lessons go only so far…Anyway, I just won't do it again.

Aaaaaah!

"Yoji!"—I was talking out loud now—"I'd do it with you!" As the words bounced around the room, I sank down to my shoulders and buried my face in what was left of the foam. "I want you!" I blubbered, though this time the bubbles muffled the words.

I climbed out of the bath, put on a clean T-shirt and shorts, and wrapped my head in a towel. When I got back to my room, I pulled the *Pulp Fiction* DVD from the shelf and checked the scene where the poor black guy says he's "pretty fucking far from okay." It wasn't LL Cool J. It was Ving Rhames. I should have known. I knew LL Cool J was a rapper. But wasn't he in some movie too? Or was he? Was this another one of my mistakes? I suppose I'm not much good at telling one black person from another. But then, I can't even tell the difference between boys I like and the ones I don't. Pretty lame.

No, I'm not lame. I'm getting my act together this time. Really.

2

There was a kid in my sixth-grade homeroom named Takashi Nizaki. He was really smart and got good grades, but at times he could be a sadistic bully and a bit schizo. He would be friends with you one day only to cut you dead the next. He was smart and good at sports, and he could talk circles around everybody, but there was something a bit spooky about him. Still, he ruled the class. The only one who could stand up to him was Masaki Urayasu from the class next door, and when Urayasu was beating the crap out of Nizaki, it was Urayasu's friend, Yoji Kaneda, who waded in to break it up.

Urayasu was really built, bulging pecs and all, and the punches he threw were on a whole different level from Nizaki's. In fact, at the moment, he was pummeling Nizaki's face—maybe because he could see how handsome it was—and each time he connected, Nizaki's head spun around, his silky hair whipping back and forth in time with the impact. The fight had started in the hall after school. Just about everybody in our class had gathered around to watch, but nobody was trying to break it up. I guess some people might have been thinking that they *should* step in—that Nizaki was a bully but he'd never really hurt anybody—but when you looked around and saw that no one else was doing anything, it seemed easier to leave it alone—let Nizaki get a little of his own medicine. That's what I thought anyway. His mistake here had been in picking his opponent—or rather in *not* picking him carefully enough. At any rate, by this point Urayasu had been beating on him for a minute straight, and Nizaki's eye was all bloody, and I thought he might go blind if it went on like this. Then I realized Nizaki was crying—right in front of everybody. It was the first time I'd seen him cry, and I'm sure that was true for everyone else too. You could feel the shock—and maybe a little bit of excitement. There was this low whistling sound every time Nizaki breathed in through his nose, and then it got all sniffly—*sususususu*—like he was having a fit or something—right in time with his shoulders heaving. He'd sort of blow the air out—*haaaaaa*—and then suck it back in—*sususususu*. His stomach bucked, and you could tell he was having trouble breathing. To tell the truth, it was an awesome sight: here was a shithead bawling his eyes out. What kind of man was he? If he was going to get the crap beat out of him *and* cry like a baby, he should never have started this in the first place. Then I realized that Kan and Shima were standing right next to me, and I wondered whether they were feeling a little sympathy for Nizaki now that he was blubbering. But then I noticed they were yelling to Urayasu to keep going! I didn't want to appear too out of it—so even though I'd been about to tell him to quit just a second before, I found myself suddenly hoping the jerk would get everything he had coming to him. I guess the real fun was thinking how hard it was going to be for him to show his face at school after this.

Urayasu went on thrashing Nizaki. Mercilessly. For whatever reason, he seemed to want to beat the last bit of shit out of him. The voices urging him on trailed off. It was getting a little scary. And Nizaki looked pretty awful—wonderfully so.

At this point a very ordinary-looking kid in a blue polo shirt—Yoji Kaneda— appeared on the scene. He wasn't particularly tall or well built.

"Give it a rest, Ura," he said. "Don't you think that's enough?"

"Not quite, Kane. I beat the shit out of this guy and he still doesn't get it."

"So why don't you leave it at that—you beat the shit out of him and he doesn't get it."

"So I'll keep on till he does get it," Urayasu said.

"Nah, that doesn't make much sense. Give it a rest."

"I know it doesn't make sense, but what the fuck!"

"Just back off a minute, how 'bout?" Urayasu had been straddling Nizaki, and as he climbed off, Kaneda patted him on the shoulder. "Pounding the crap out of a guy is hard work. Look at your hands—they're all torn up."

Urayasu glanced down at his raw, red knuckles.

"Shit! I fucked up my hands."

"And they'll know you were fighting if you go to the nurse's office," Kaneda added. "Just go wash up," he said, sending Urayasu off in the direction of the boys' room. When he was gone, Kaneda turned to Nizaki, who was still sobbing on the floor, and reached out his arm to help him up.

His long, slender, beautiful arm.

I can still remember exactly how it looked: the delicate joints at the elbow and wrist, the graceful taper so completely different from Urayasu's beefy knob. As if something wonderful—an angel's wing—had been called in to replace something awful—a pig's foot maybe. That's how it looked to me, anyway.

Cowering on the floor, Nizaki covered his face with his hands and kicked at the outstretched hand.

"Leave me alone!" he blubbered. "What do you think this is?"

To which the boy in the blue polo shirt replied quite simply: "It's love."

Yoji Kaneda was always game for anything, and he was always, always doing something stupid. He told me himself that he and a friend once pissed out the bus window on a field trip in elementary school (though he swore they didn't hit anybody, not even any cars), and another time, on field day, he ran the hundred meters holding a badminton racquet, telling everybody he needed a handicap. He even ran a relay the same way. (He came in first in the hundred; in the relay, baton in one hand and racquet in the other, he managed to catch one runner on another team but then got the racquet caught between his legs and went sprawling.) And now, he'd said "It's love," and even though he added something stupid like "Love will save the world," the word was still left hanging there. It was the first time I'd ever heard someone say the word so raw, just like that, and somehow it made me feel embarrassed. The first character of my name—the "ai" in Aiko— means "love." But I'd hardly ever heard anyone use the word *except* in my name. And now I realized that nobody had been forcing me to stand there and watch Nizaki get the daylights beat out of him. It must have hurt, and it must have been a shock to be beat up in front of people like that. It would be for anybody. So it would have been natural enough, right at the start, to tell Urayasu to stop or do something to end it. You don't stand around worrying that kids will think you have a crush on Nizaki; as soon as you realize it's time to stop it, you speak right up and say something. My name may mean "love child," but I seem to have a little deficit where the love's concerned, and I sure as hell am never going to save any world. At least not like this.

All of sudden, I couldn't stand being there anymore and walked away. Kan and Shima stayed behind—apparently they really were infatuated with Nizaki, in a way.

As I left them and headed down the hall, I ran into Urayasu and some of his buddies coming out of the bathroom. His hands were still wet, the skin red and raw around his knuckles. "Shit! That hurts!" he was muttering. As I walked by, I gave him a "you asshole" kind of look, but when I thought about it I realized I was just as much of an asshole. Maybe more. Urayasu had been mad about something, and that's why he pulverized Nizaki. But what was my excuse for standing there watching them?

I didn't give a damn about Nizaki one way or the other. He only bullied boys, so I was safe, and though he was cute enough in a way, he wasn't my type. His bullying was carefully planned and totally vicious, but he wasn't as violent about it as some of the other kids. There were meaner bullies who did worse things.

Then why had I let him get beat up without trying to help? Why had I stood by and watched him get smashed to a pulp?

Clearly, I wanted to see him suffer. Physically and psychologically.

Not that I had any particular reason. That's just how I felt at the moment. Nizaki had bullied everyone else without ever having to pay the price, so this just seemed like the right time for him to get what was coming to him—as though it was finally his turn. I guess that's just the way it is with bullying: what goes around comes around. There was this time in fourth grade when everybody in the class suddenly decided to pretend I didn't exist. I never knew why, but I suppose there's really no such thing as a reason when it comes to bullying. What goes around comes around. So I'm sure I just felt that the needle had spun and finally pointed at Nizaki.

But why do you suppose there's bullying in the first place?

Because there's not enough love, I guess.

Who doesn't have enough love?
Me?
Everybody?
The whole world?

And not enough love for who?
For me?
For everyone?
For the world?
Or for Nizaki?

I have no idea.
Even now, I really don't.
That evening, the day I first noticed Yoji Kaneda, I went home from school, had dinner, took a bath, and watched TV. Then at some point I wrote this sad little line in my diary: "Not enough love! Not near enough."

Whose love? For who?
Who knew? Even now, I don't know.
But some important stuff came out of all this: I found Yoji Kaneda, I started thinking about love for the first time in my life, and I had drilled into my brain the image of that pale, slender arm extending out of that blue polo shirt, reaching out for Nizaki as he lay there on the floor, bawling his eyes out in front of everybody.

Still, I didn't suddenly feel like I was head-over-heels, out-of-my-mind in love with Yoji.
Like I said before, he was a bit of a lightweight. He was like a baby monkey, always doing this weird stuff. To be honest, he

wasn't exactly the type of guy who was likely to be a love object for a sixth-grade girl on the brink of puberty. Not the type at all.

And after the Nizaki incident, it was mostly that dumbass side of Yoji that I saw around school. Once during a soccer game in gym class, he suddenly turned on his own team and kicked a goal into their net, winning the game for the other side. His teammates chased him around, and somehow he wound up on the roof of the gym. The coach was madder than hell when he found out. And once on a field trip to one of those deer parks, he tried to bring a fawn on the bus. When they told him he couldn't, the poor thing ran after the bus halfway back to school. Then there was the time when a bunch of his buddies were goofing off in class, scribbling stuff on each others' faces, and the teacher made Yoji stand in the hall during free period with "toilet" on his forehead, "hot dog" on one cheek, and "Nagoya" on the other.

Way dumb.

Around that same time, I started reading grown-up magazines like *Olive* and *Seventeen*, started shaving my legs and armpits and plucking my brows. A boy who acted like that wouldn't have made much of an impression. Still, he was always somewhere in the back of my mind, even as I was only registering his dumbass side.

I guess it was true even then. Whenever I wasn't in class, I was looking for him—during free period or when we were mopping the halls, on the way to school or on the way home. At the time I think I told myself that he was always good for a laugh, that I just wanted to see the next stupid thing he would do. I guess I paid so much attention to him because that expectation was so often rewarded.

But whatever.

One of the necessary conditions for falling in love is that you simply *see* the other person often enough. If you see him enough, you begin to notice his good qualities.

Good qualities?

He's an asshole and a goofball.

He seems to have a need to be noticed. (Which is something I hate.)

He's loud. (Which is another thing I hate.)

And he's short.

Oh, did I forget to mention that? I'm on the tall side, and by sixth grade I was already five feet three inches and completely uninterested in any boy who wasn't at least my height. So you can see that there was no chance I'd fall for a runt like Kaneda. None.

But somehow I did.

It didn't matter that he was a short, loud, conspicuous asshole clown. Somehow I was suddenly flipped by the hand of "love," by that pale arm.

But how?

How did that one word, *love,* and that one outstretched arm so totally get to me?

Was I that desperate?

I don't think so. I really don't.

Or was I? After all, I did write those words in my diary: "Not enough love! Not near enough." But that was about bullying—not about romance.

But love isn't selective like that; it's universal, all-encompassing.

That last bit was Kerstin, who had reappeared again from somewhere.

So Yoji was reaching his hand out to you too, as someone who was part of Nizaki's world. Deep down, you know it instinctively— that if you grabbed hold of that hand and held on to it, you could have gone to a "Love will save the world" kind of place.

That's nonsense.

It's not, and we're not talking about Kaneda when he was a kid.

So I'm not in love with Yoji in a romantic way? I just want someone to save me from my world?

Not "just." Though that is part of it.

Part of it? What else is there?

Well, there's "liking."

"Liking"?

It makes no sense to ask what "liking" is; it's a meaningless question.

I'm lost.

"Like" is "like"—that's all. There's no reason about it. No other side to the story. "I like it here." "I like this kind of place." You can say those kinds of things, but you can't say, "I like it because there is this place" or "I like it because there is such a place."

I still don't follow.

Because I don't know how to say it right. But you know what I mean.

I do.

That's right.

I had watched Yoji doing all that stupid stuff and told myself over and over what an idiot he was, yet somehow, still, I fell in love with him.

There was no particular reason—just opportunity.

That slender, pale, outstretched hand.

Such a beautiful hand.

And the "Love will save the world" part.

But I'm pretty sure that when somebody falls in love, it's not about this quality or that habit or this feeling or doing something that way—you fall in love with something that's deep inside the other person, like a core or a nucleus, right at the heart, no strings attached. I know, you see, because Yoji's core stuck inside me, and it won't come off.

3

I thought about skipping school, but I didn't want to be behind the curve when Sano started spreading his lies. I wanted to be ready to respond, to make my case early and often. Still, when I got to school it seemed as though he had got the jump on me with his texting. It was already too late. It would be brutal now.

As soon as I walked into the classroom, Kan and Shima stopped me. They had something they wanted to talk about, told me to come with them—and not out onto the balcony or on the stairs or in the hall in front of the art room, but in the *bathroom*. Which I knew was scary, but before I could even answer, Narucchi and Miyon and Nakajima and even Maki had followed us in and gathered around the mirror. Narucchi and Maki weren't even at the party last night. If Kan and Shima were bringing in girls who had nothing to do with anything, this wasn't some little thing; this was a big deal. And then there was Maki. Major scary. If she was here, I was in for the full treatment.

But why was she here?

They were planning to do it right. No, I didn't really know whether they were all after me. But if they were, I was pretty sure there wasn't much I could do about it.

Shit!

But you've got to keep calm, Aiko. Keep cool.

Why were you suddenly the target? And what were you going to do about it? How could you fight back against so many girls? Or maybe you should admit you did whatever it was they thought you did and just apologize—though how do you apologize if you don't know what you did?

You were about to be drawn and quartered, and you weren't even sure what the charges were. As they'd been leading me into the bathroom, I'd wracked my brain, but I still had no idea. What was this all about?

Was it because I did it with Akihiko Sano? But lots of other girls did too. Kan and Miyon at least. Last year or the year before. The only reason I wanted to try him was because they'd said he was so fantastically awesome. "Sano's a sex machine!" I'm quoting them here. So why were they after me now for actually doing it with him? It made no sense. Because I didn't get in touch after I disappeared with Sano from the party last night? But when I left with him they must have known what we were going to do. No one said anything at the time, and it wasn't the first time I'd left a party with some guy, so it shouldn't have made any difference.

So maybe I did something at the party? I don't remember much.

Or maybe before the party? Not likely.

So what then?

Why was I here in the bathroom? Why was I suddenly the target of the bully court?

I still didn't know, but I didn't have any more time to think about it. Miyon, who was standing next to Maki, spoke up first. "You probably know why we've called you here," she said. No, no idea. Why? When I didn't answer, Shima broke in. "Speak up," she ordered. "Say something, Aiko. We don't like your attitude." If I said I didn't know, they might take it wrong or someone might think I was being a smart-ass—worse still if that someone was Maki. But I had taken too long thinking this over. Out of nowhere came a slap to the side of my face. "Speak up, Aiko!" Maki shouted. I was shocked more than hurt. What did she think she was doing? So I shot back, "What the *fuck* do you think you're doing?" and kicked out with my right leg, catching her in the thigh. And it worked, a bit anyway: Maki crumpled. I was in pretty good shape

from kendo and tennis, and the kick must've hurt. She rubbed her
thigh and muttered, "You think that hurt, bitch?" "You think I give
a fuck?" I retorted, and as I did, I jumped on her, pushing her head
down with the weight of my body and at the same time bringing
my leg up. *Gaaannn!* I could feel her face smashing against my
knee. It was a move my brother taught me. He had also taught
me what to do when I was way outnumbered like this: he said you
should try to take out the strongest one right away. Which is why
I had gone after Maki. I grabbed her hair and smashed my knee
into her pretty face over and over. "Wait wai…shit," she gurgled.
"Stop! Ouch! OUCH! SHIT! OUCH!" I saw something red on
the bathroom tiles and knew Maki was bleeding from the nose,
but I kept on cracking her face against my knee.

She was totally scary as far as I was concerned. We had a term
for this kind of group ambush; we called it the Death Penalty—
and Maki was known as the Executioner. The flavor of the day
was the "Crucifixion," which was the bathroom version they had
planned for me: these really thin, sterile needles were run through
the palms of both hands to nail the victim to the door of one of
the stalls. There were other penalties, all with catchy names—the
Butt Drill Tour, the Safety Pin Tattoo—but the Crucifixion was
as scary as any. Actually, it was mostly the guys who used it, but
Maki was just mean enough to want to try it.

A bunch of stuff went through my head as I was kneeing her
face: no needles or hammer…but got to pound Maki…make
sure she can't fight back…but what was happening?…why were
they doing this? I knew that the other girls weren't like Maki,
that I could probably talk my way out of this if it was just them.
Anyway, when they saw what I was doing to Maki, they would
probably back off. Which is why I was kicking the shit out of her
right there in front of them. "You're out of your league, Maki," I

shouted at her. "You little shit! You're totally fucked!" The fights
in girl manga were never like this, so I had to use stuff I'd read
in guy comics, sound effects and all. Maki couldn't talk anymore,
just sputter. "*Ahh, ahh, kaa, gaa.*" The other girls were telling me
to stop now, but of course no one actually stepped in to break
it up. Chickenshits. No surprise. They yelled at me, and I kept
on kneeing Maki in the face, smashing it up; but then suddenly
they all drew back in a circle and got real quiet, so I slowly let
go of her. Her nose had been bleeding all this time, so her face
was completely red and gross. My thigh was red too, and there
was a little blood on my skirt. As I let go of her, she slumped to
the floor, but she put her arms down to catch herself; I suppose
because she didn't want to end up flat out on the bathroom tiles.
She gasped or gagged or something and then tried to crawl out
the bathroom door on her hands and knees. But I pulled her hair
from behind and sat her down right by the door. "Where do you
think you're going?" I said. "Have a seat." There was this little turn
in the passage that led from the bathroom out to the hall, so the
kids passing by out there couldn't see her. She sat, bloody face
buried in her knees. It was like a scene straight out of a horror
flick. Her shoulders were heaving, and it didn't look like she'd be
getting up for a while.

Hiding my fear, I turned to face Miyon and the others.

They had all drawn back away from me, as far as they could
get, and they looked a little nervous. Not scared exactly, but I was
getting some kind of strange vibe. What? Why were they looking
at me like that?

"What?"

"You're a little scary, Aiko," Shima said.

"What do you mean?"

"Why did you do that to Maki? She just slapped you—you

went way ape-shit."

Ape-shit? There were six of them and one of me, and they were planning to crucify me. Here in the bathroom, with Maki as executioner—and *I* went ape-shit? If I hadn't put her out of commission once and for all, if I'd left her anything to hit back with, I would have got double in return. She would have crucified me for sure, or worse.

"You brought her into this, you shits," I said. They said nothing. I was done with them. No more partying with Kan or Shima or Miyon or Nakajima or Narucchi. Crucifixion in the bathroom, with Maki—that was the end. And then to try to make me out as the bad guy on top of that? No, that was too much. Way much. But fuck it. Whatever. I still had some friends. Yoshida and Marilyn. But I was done with this crowd. Though before I stopped talking to them forever, there was one more thing I had to do: find out why they were doing this.

So I just asked: "Why are you doing this?" I really wanted to know. Why had they suddenly hauled me off to the bathroom to crucify me? When we'd made plans to do all sorts of fun stuff together this summer, go to the beach and shit. Which we would *not* be doing now. Why was that? Why?

But they ignored my question and instead Kan asked one of her own.

"Aiko, where were you last night?"

Last night?

"I was home," I said. What did she mean? Did they want me to tell them I'd gone to a hotel with Sano?

"But you left with Sano," Kan said. "Where'd you go?"

Was this for real? They wanted to know about that?

"Who the fuck cares where I was," I told her.

"We do!"

"Why should you? And why should I have to tell you?"

"You went to a hotel, didn't you? Did you really go home last night?"

"Go ask Sano, if you're so curious."

And then they all stood there for a minute, staring at me with these weird looks.

What the fuck?

"But Sano didn't come to school. Nobody's seen him since last night. They're saying he's dead. Murdered. You didn't know?"

What the fuck?

"What the fuck?"

"That's right. That's what we're asking you. What the fuck?" And with that they began closing in on me, and now their faces were real serious. Though I wasn't sure that serious meant they were really serious...but whatever. I didn't understand anything that was going on. What did they mean "murdered"? What the fuck? It probably wasn't a "what the fuck" kind of moment, but I really didn't have a clue. What the fuck?

"How was he killed?" I asked.

"That's what we'd like to know," Shima shot back. "And were you involved?" Kan added.

"Hold on," I said. "Is he really dead? Is this for real?"

"Would we be here now if it weren't?" Narucchi said. "We don't know for sure that he's dead, but we know he disappeared."

So just "disappeared." Vanished, like the assistant in a magician's trick? Then he's more "missing person" than "murdered" person.

"So, like I said," I said, "hold on a minute. I don't understand a thing you're telling me. Start from the beginning. How did Sano disappear?"

But Kan cut me off. "Forget it. We don't have time for your questions. We want answers. You tell us, Aiko, where were you last night from ten to eleven?"

"I got home at ten-thirty and didn't go out after that."

"But where were you between ten and ten-thirty?"

"I was on the train home from Shinjuku."

"The express from Shinjuku to Chofu takes fifteen minutes…"

"But I waited at Shinjuku and the train was a little late, and I had to walk home from the station. What are you saying?"

"Were you by yourself?"

"By myself?"

"Did you go home alone?"

"Of course!"

"And Sano?"

"He wasn't with me."

"So what happened to him?"

"How should I know? I got sick of him and left him at the hotel."

"So you left him at the hotel! Why?"

"Like I said, I got sick of him, he's disgusting!"

"Sick of him how?"

"Who cares? I left him there."

"We care! Somebody killed him. What do you mean you got sick of him?"

Killed him? You just said you didn't know whether he was dead or not! All you really know is that he's missing.

"Wait a minute! You don't think I did it, do you?"

"We don't know who did it," Kan said.

"You don't know, but you think it was me."

"We're just trying to get the facts. Innocent until proven guilty."

"What the—Why would I want to kill Sano?"

"You just said you got sick of him." It was Shima this time. "So if you couldn't stand him, you might have killed him. That's like a motive or something."

"And you're like a moron or something. Do you kill everybody you can't stand?"

Narucchi jumped in to defend her. "Shima wouldn't kill anybody. It's you we're talking about, Aiko," she said, and then all of us, me included, turned to look at Maki, who was still sitting on the floor, head down, pressing her handkerchief against her nose.

"Maki," Kan said, "you should look up—the bleeding stops faster." Maki shook her head but said nothing. It was obvious she was crying and didn't want us to see her covered with blood and tears and snot.

Okay, point taken. I'm good in a fight. And I guess I did kick Sano in the face last night…

Whoa! It felt like somebody had just kicked *me*.

Now that you mention it, I *did* kick him in the face. Kicked him—*sugaaan!*—and knocked him flat on the floor.

But he laughed about it afterward. "Ouch!" he'd said. But then he giggled. But what if that kick was harder than I realized or I'd hit him in the wrong place? What if he'd started bleeding inside that stupid head of his? What if it got worse later and he died?

I felt the blood draining out of my head, my face going white. They were all staring at me, still looking funny. But wait a MINUTE! It's not what you think. It was just one little kick. Nobody ever killed a boy with one little kick!

But Sano was pretty scrawny. And my kick did get him pretty much straight in the face…

No, no, no! People aren't that fragile! Nobody croaks from one girl-kick.

I was now completely tongue-tied, unable to think about anything but my kick. I was almost too frightened to speak. Somewhere in the back of my head a white guy was telling me all that stuff they say when they arrest you: "You have the right to remain silent; you have the right to an attorney…" Had I really killed Sano? I sure hadn't meant to. This was *not* premeditated. Murder in the second degree? Involuntary manslaughter? But hold on, we don't even know whether he's dead or not!

"Say something, Aiko!"

"Did you remember something, Aiko?"

"Tell us, Aiko!"

"I didn't do anything," I finally managed to mutter, but this only threw gas on the fire.

"Didn't do what? Tell us everything!"

"Don't be stupid! Tell us!"

"What happened last night?"

"Why did you get so mad at him?"

Shut up shut up shut up shut UP!

Kan finally seemed to realize what was going on. "She can't answer if we're all yelling at her," she said. "Quiet, girls." Then she turned to me. "So tell us what happened, Aiko. I don't know why you got so mad at him, but you did. So did you also beat the shit out of him like you did Maki just now?"

No!

It wasn't anything like Maki.

But it also wasn't true that I didn't know what I'd done to him—so I decided to exercise my right to remain silent.

But then they were all over me again, trying to get me to confess. And I knew if I told them I'd only kicked him in the face, they'd never let up. Then a girl came into the bathroom—a little awkward with the would-be Crucifixion in progress. Of course the new girl would need to know what was going on, and this forced Kan to backtrack a bit.

"So, Aiko, tell us. What happened with you and Sano?"

"Katsura and Sano?" The new girl—Riko or Emiri or

something—was suddenly all ears. I wanted to tell them nothing had happened, that I had nothing to do with Sano, but I wasn't so sure myself anymore. My legs felt weak, and I was shaking.

"Aiko, don't you have anything to say for yourself?" Even Nakada was getting into the act, though there was a smirk on her face. But I didn't—have anything to say for myself, not at the moment.

Then, as I stood there, more girls started coming in—it was a restroom, after all—and when they realized they had walked into a Crucifixion-in-progress, they didn't want to leave. So the place got crowded and crazy, and that, in the end, was what saved me.

Because suddenly, Yoji Kaneda came wading into the circle of girls, shouting, "What's going on in here?" I wasn't at my best, but here he was anyway—in the girls' room. He ignored the screams for him to get out and pushed through to find me covered in blood—Maki's blood—in the middle of the crowd. "What do you think you're doing?"

"Shut up!" Kan shouted, trying to drown him out.

"No, you shut up! What were you going to do to her? No, don't tell me: you were going to crucify her because of Sano. But do you know how crazy that sounds? Did you know that somebody sent a toe to Sano's house?"

A shock ran through the room.

Through me too.

A toe?

You mean somebody cut off his toe?

And sent it to his house?

But I wasn't the only one who hadn't known. "No!" someone gasped, and then everybody started to scream all at once.

"You didn't know?" Yoji said, a puzzled look on his face. "Maybe I wasn't supposed to mention it. Forget I said anything! I'll be in trouble for sure." He sounded like an idiot, but he had managed to deflect attention from me. The girls started pressing him for details, but he just laughed. "No, no. Forget I said anything. Ask the cops. But no more bullying people like this. You're finished here." So saying, he grabbed me by the arm and dragged me out of the bathroom. In the confusion, they couldn't stop him. Bye, Kan. Bye, Miyon. Narucchi. Nakajima, Shima. They had all been such good friends...

Yoji pulled me down the hall. When he finally let go of my hand, I realized where we were. The nurse's office. Why? Then I remembered the blood on my knee.

"You should let them look at that," he said. I felt my face go red, but there was nothing to do but tell the truth.

"That's not my blood, Yoji."

"It's not? Whose is it?"

"Maki's."

"Maki? Maki Saito? How? Why?"

"It's a long story..."

"Was she in the bathroom?"

"I think she's still there." A lot of girls had wandered in and out, and I wasn't exactly sure.

"Then I'm going back to see if she's okay. But what did you do to her, Katsura?"

"I guess I hurt her."

"You stupid—You stay here and think about what you've done," he said, laying the palm of his hand on my forehead for a moment, as if miming a slap. Then he turned and ran off down the hall. I could hear him bounding up the stairs two at a time.

And then I didn't know how to feel.

Happy? Sad? Both at once?

He had saved me, which was a good thing...

I would just leave it at that.

I guess.

But there I was, abandoned outside the nurse's office, and as I was standing there thinking about what to do next, this teacher—I didn't know his name—came bolting down the hall. Not good! I was sure he'd say something to me, but then he passed right by, ignoring me. He pounded on the door to the nurse's office and then opened it. And as he did, I caught sight of Maki inside. She had made it out of the bathroom ahead of me and come straight here. There she sat with a big patch of gauze taped to her nose—at least it looked really big compared to her tiny face. The tape was still white, but the gauze was already bright red. From either side, her eyes were looking out—right at me. It was like they were shooting some invisible laser, and when it hit me, my heart stopped.

In the two terrifying seconds before my life ended, I knew with complete certainty that Maki and her shattered nose would follow me into the next life and spend eternity devising the proper punishment for my crime.

But what was the appropriate punishment for destroying an absolutely perfect nose—a nose a model would kill to have?

Would I get to pick it myself?

4

A lot of other stuff happened, and when it was all over, and night had come and I was in bed, curled up there in the dark, I suddenly realized that someone was standing at the foot of my bed—Sano! But not exactly. A pale, white Sano face was floating silently above me, bending low, reaching out for my bare feet. He took hold of my left ankle with an iron grip, but his hand was icy cold, and I realized he must be dead. I wanted to cry out, but I couldn't. What was he doing? But almost as soon as this question occurred to me, I realized he was pulling a single white thread from the arch of my left foot, a thick piece of cotton thread that somehow seemed to be coming from my body. It seemed to come from somewhere inside my chest, through my body, to my left foot. And Sano seemed to be pulling it out of me, *monyomonyomonyosui!* It felt as though the thread were wound around my guts, and as he pulled, my insides dissolved into mush. First my stomach. My belly seemed to be getting hot and slowly melting. As my lungs unraveled and shrank, my breathing grew shallow. My organs seemed to be dissolving one after the other, and my body shriveled wherever one disappeared. Then I realized my heart was melting, and I panicked. Sano's blank face made me feel sick with fear. I wanted to tell him to stop, to get out of my room, but my body had gone limp. Then the thread began to empty out my neck, and I couldn't even turn to look at him. I lay on my back, staring up at the dark ceiling. I would die. Sano would empty me and I would die. My body would unravel into a single strand, and I would die. A single, long, white thread.

What would become of me? I had no idea.

I had no idea, but I was suddenly really sad and I began to cry. I wanted to be able to cry for just a moment before I became a thread. My tears would wet the thread. They would be absorbed by the thick cotton, and that would at least feel good.

The unraveling continued, climbing from my neck to my brain, which was slowly turning to thread. Soon I wouldn't be able to think—so what should be my last thought?

Of course! A memory. Of someone I loved.

Yoji Kaneda.

I thought about Yoji's face. When my brain was nothing but a white thread, it would probably fall to the earth in a shape that matched Yoji's profile.

But, hold on a minute…

Wait!

What?

What did he look like?

No! It couldn't be!

I really couldn't remember what he looked like.

Yoji.

Yoji.

Yoji.

Shit no! I couldn't remember at all.

Yoji.

Yoji.

Yoji.

Nope. I was going to become nothing but thread, but for the life of me I couldn't remember.

Had every bit of Yoji, every memory, turned to thread?

No, really?

I wanted to see his face one more time.

Yoji!

Pitch black, and I'm still having this nightmare—nothing but the sound of the thread unraveling in my head, and the feeling that it's being reeled in through the sole of my foot. But when I open my eyes it's already morning…or later…The light coming in through the crack in the curtains looks suspiciously bright.

Definitely one of the worst five nightmares of all time.

The top of the list, though, the worst one of all time, I was at this funeral with all these people sitting around me, and I realized it was my brother's funeral. But just as that was sinking in, the guy who had killed him showed up and started attacking all the mourners. I ran off at top speed, but he ran after me. He was catching up with me when I suddenly noticed Miyuki, the little girl who lives next door—she really does, in real life—so I shoved her toward him. When I turned around again, she was all bloody and screaming hysterically, but I kept on running…

That was one creepy nightmare. And even though it was only a dream, I still feel guilty whenever I see Miyuki walking by on her way to school. In the dream I knew exactly what I was doing: I was sacrificing Miyuki to that monster to save my own skin.

I guess I'm just a cruel bitch. Scratch away the surface and you get someone who'd throw her own sister or the little girl next door under the train to save herself.

I lay on my bed and twisted my left foot around so I could see the arch. No thread. Duh. But I was still relieved. There was something too creepy about the idea of becoming just a long piece of string. Spine-tingling, as they say.

I felt exhausted and decided to stay in bed for a while. So as I lay there, I tried to remember Yoji's face. Bingo! I could see him there in front of the nurse's office after he'd rescued me from the bathroom, worrying about my bloody knee. I remembered!

But why was that?

How could I remember something when I was awake that I couldn't recall when I was asleep?

It was all the same brain, but it seemed like a completely different organ when I was sleeping. Maybe it was. Could your brain be one way when you're awake and then become totally another when you're sleeping?

Or maybe there were two brains.

One for when you were awake, and another for when you were asleep?

No, that's too weird.

Your brain—my brain—is probably just a little fuzzy when you're asleep, so it can do some really weird things but forget how to do the simple, obvious tasks. It can imagine you being stretched out into a really long string, but it can't remember the face of the boy you like. Love. Which really sucks.

Maybe what I need to do is carve Yoji's face deeper into my brain so that a little thing like falling asleep won't make me forget him again. What if sometime something really terrible happens and I'm just about to lose consciousness, or even dying or something, and what if, just as I'm blacking out, I can't remember how he looks?

I need to be able to remember Yoji easily and quickly.

But how?

Well, you might start by seeing him again, Aiko.

You've got a point, Kerstin.

So I grabbed my phone from the table by the bed and checked the time. Ten minutes after noon. Lunchtime. Flat on my stomach, cheek on my pillow, I jot off a text.

Good morning! Just woke up. Eating lunch? Want to skip class and go somewhere? Go where? He'd want to know. "To find out about Sano or something." Then he'd probably ask how we'd do that. "I'm not sure how, but there must be something we can do. Anyway, we should meet."

I was pretty sure he wouldn't refuse. He was a good guy. Sano was an asshole, but Yoji was always nice, even to him. So if there was any way he could manage it, he would try to help. He almost never skipped class, but he would probably even do that if I asked him. Come to think of it, he must have been skipping yesterday when he rescued me. I remember once, in the middle of some class, he stuck his hand up and said he felt dizzy. He ran out of the room and never came back. He's a serious guy, but he knows how to handle himself when he's got more important things to do.

I added to the text: *I have an idea about what happened to Sano.*

And it was true, I did have an idea—sort of. I wondered how much this would interest Yoji.

Akihiko Sano had stayed another half hour after I left the hotel. Then he'd gone downstairs, stopped at the front desk to pay the bill, and had vanished. Nobody knew where he'd gone after that, but he never got home—that much was certain. Though we did know what had happened to his toe. At some point during the night, a package had been left at his house. His mother discovered it early the next morning, and when she opened it, she found the little toe from his right foot covered in plastic wrap and sealed in a baggie. And a note demanding ten million yen in ransom if they ever wanted to see their son alive again.

That's what I learned from the detective who came by to ask me about going to the love hotel with Sano that night.

Then I realized there was something familiar about all this, about sending a toe to a victim's house. I'd seen it before. But where? A movie. One with that gross guy in it, and with that other even grosser guy. And something about bowling, and a man in some kind of purple outfit dancing around in slow motion after he gets a strike. What was it?—directed by the something-or-other brothers. A rich old guy's wife gets kidnapped and they send her toe to the husband. And then the bowling, and then somehow bowling and kidnapping get all mixed up. What was it called?

Oh! And Buscemi was in it too! Steve Buscemi! I've been a huge Buscemi fan ever since *Con Air*—something about that long, lanky frame and those big round eyes, that loose mouth, he just gets to me. Buscemi, Buscemi.

The Coen Brothers.

That's it! *The Hudsucker Proxy*!

No, that wasn't it. I checked the old movie programs on my bookshelf, and it turned out that Tim Robbins was in *The Hudsucker Proxy*, not Steve Buscemi. The movie about bowling and kidnapping was *The Big Lebowski*. Jeff Bridges played Buscemi's gross friend, and John Goodman was the really gross fat guy, and the weird guy who danced after getting the strike was John Turturro. How could I have been so far off?

John Goodman was *so* gross in *The Big Lebowski* that I didn't even buy the program—shit! It would have come in handy about now. But I remember, I'm sure of it. This lady gets kidnapped, and they cut off her toe and send it to her stinking-rich husband. But I don't remember how it all turned out.

I seem to remember that John gave this crazy speech about something.

…And?…that the kidnapping was all a fake.

But I don't really remember the ending.

I'll have to rent the DVD. Maybe I can watch it with Yoji. That would be fun.

Like a date.

But I shouldn't be thinking about that right now. A guy I did it with—even if it was just once!—has been kidnapped. I have to be more serious.

But just then a text came from Yoji. *Skipping class. Looking for Sano with Kita, Shiba & Satoru. Where are you? Got things we want to ask you.*

What? What was he doing with those boys? My phone started ringing, and Yoji's name came on the display. I tossed it on the bed. What good was he if he came with *Kita, Shiba & Satoru*? We had to be one-on-one—anything else was *claustrophobic*.

The ringtone—from *Life is Beautiful*—played all the way through, twice. It stopped for a minute, and then, just as I went to put away *The Hudsucker Proxy* program, it started playing again—*dadadadadada*. It played a couple more times, then stopped.

Now that it was quiet again, I picked up the phone, erased the incoming messages, and put it away in my bag. Then I put on a bra, T-shirt, and jeans, pulled up my hair and fastened it with a clip, put on my glasses, combed my bangs, put on some lip gloss, picked up my bag, and left. I was going to get *The Big Lebowski*, even if I had to watch it alone. Maybe the movie would offer some kind of clue to Sano's disappearance.

But even after I got back and watched the DVD, my opinion hadn't changed: John Goodman is really gross. He's fat and he doesn't listen to anybody, and he says all this dumb stuff, all of which is wrong and screws everything up—and still he's clueless. So I really can't stand him. But I was right: Steve Buscemi as Donny is really cute. He gets killed somehow or other at the end, but he has this excellent, Buscemiesque way of dying.

Any—way! The point is the kidnapping. Kidnapping. In the end, the kidnapping in the movie is a fake. They haven't really kidnapped the wife at all. They just cut off the toe of a woman in the kidnappers' gang and sent it to the rich husband. And it turns out he's tired of his wife anyway and realizes he could use the kidnapping to get rid of her. But he has to *seem* like he's worried about her, so he hires Lewbowski—aka Jeff Bridges—the biggest slacker in LA, to make the payoff to the kidnappers. He's pretty sure Lewbowski will fuck things up and get her killed. That's when John Goodman gets involved and things get really screwed up, and everybody gets totally disgusted, the kidnappers, the rich guy—and me too.

When the movie was over, I thought for a while. Was Sano's
kidnapping based on *The Big Lebowski*?

What if we assumed the kidnapping was a fake?

That left you with two possibilities right off the bat. One was
what John Goodman's idiot character was thinking: the victim
had staged it herself—or himself. In other words, Sano had faked
his own kidnapping. But then you had the problem of the toe.
John Goodman kept saying the wife had cut off her own toe and
sent it to her husband, but that's a dumbass theory at best. Even
an idiot like Sano wouldn't go around cutting off his own toe. So
he must have found someone else's toe to send. But whose?

But supposing he did find somebody, it still would have made
the toe donor pretty mad, so you can assume there was a big fight
over the donation. But maybe it didn't stop there. Maybe Sano
killed the owner of the toe and cut it off? Then he was guilty of
murder in addition to faking a kidnapping…But hold on, that
seemed all backwards. Who'd commit a murder in order to fake
a kidnapping? Maybe he murdered the guy first and then came
up with the idea of staging the kidnapping—that made more
sense. That's probably it: he committed murder and then faked
the kidnapping to cover it up.

Of course! That way he'd have the ransom money to start a
new life on the run. If he didn't reappear after the ransom was
paid, everybody would assume the kidnappers had killed him and
gotten rid of the body—and after a while everybody would give
up looking for him, and he could live happily ever after, someplace
faraway where nobody knew him. And if he got tired of happily
ever after, he could always go home and say it had taken him
all that time to escape from the kidnappers. It was foolproof!—
for a really good liar anyway. So this was a much cooler plot: kill

somebody and fake a kidnapping to cover it up! The whole movie scenario was writing itself in my head…

But hold on a minute, Aiko. Calm down. That's the first hypothesis. What about number two? Which was just like what happened in *The Big Lebowski*. Sano suddenly disappears, and somebody else decides to make it look like a kidnapping in order to collect the ransom. But who was that somebody?

Who knew?

I didn't know much about Sano's friends, but it had to be somebody who knew him well enough to hear right away that he hadn't come home that night.

Sano's friends? He had lots, boys and girls, so there were plenty of suspects. It made my brain hurt to think about it.

And the toe was still a problem. I decided to think about that again for a while. If someone else was involved, where'd he get a toe?

It was the same deal: no one was going to smile sweetly while you cut off his toe, so there was still a major battle with whoever wanted to fake the kidnapping. And maybe he got killed and it turned into murder again. But it still didn't make sense to commit murder just to fake a kidnapping, so you had to turn it around again and figure someone else besides Sano had committed murder and then staged the kidnapping to get ransom money in order to disappear. Could be. Or maybe not.

Or there was still another possibility: one of Sano's friends had killed somebody and then Sano had agreed to help that kid by faking the kidnapping. You couldn't put it past Sano to come up with the idea of trying to get ransom money out of his own parents.

No, maybe not. That seemed like a stretch.

Okay, then suppose Sano did it all himself, and once he had the money he gave it to his friend to run away with. That way he could later show up at home spouting crap about how the kidnappers had let him go. That was possible too, wasn't it?

But now I had a bunch of maybes and no way to figure out which theory made the most sense. Maybe it was better that way—allow for all the possibilities to be true at once. Or something like that. Anyway, I was pretty sure it was a case of Lebowski—the kidnapping was a fake. But then didn't it also make sense that the murder had come first?…

Probably.

All of that assumes, though, that it's impossible to cut off your own toe. But is it? If you were getting ten million yen, couldn't you part with one little toe?

Maybe. I bet I could, under the right circumstances. Ten million yen for one toe. Pretty decent trade. All you had to do, aside from cutting it off, was write a scary note, send it with the toe, collect the ransom—and go home. Mission accomplished.

Even better: if your mom and dad put the toe in the freezer and you got home real quick, you might even be able to get to the hospital and have it sewn back on.

In that case, for that one second of pain, you'd have the ransom money *and* your toe.

Nice! Who couldn't stand a little pain for that? You'd be singing all the way to the bank. Given the chance, anybody would do it. Shit, I could do it right now!

Ten million yen. You could buy a whole lot of stuff with that.

For the next half hour I flipped through *Olive* and *Spring* and some of the other magazines I had on my shelf, thinking about what I could buy with that kind of money.

That's when Yoji showed up.

5

"Not much going on, I see!" he said. And then, "What did you think you were doing, messing up Maki like that? How could you screw up the prettiest face in the class?" Then he laughed. I suppose it did bother him a little that I'd hurt Maki, but I doubted he was really blaming me. He had figured out right away in the bathroom that they intended to crucify me. So he had rescued me, then went back to help Maki, and now was able to laugh about it and make the whole thing into a joke—mostly to make me feel better. Pretty sweet. And shy too. When he'd left me at the nurse's office, pretending to be worried about Maki, it wasn't really her he was thinking of. He knew what hell my school life would be if everybody found out that I had taken on a popular girl like Maki, even to avoid crucifixion. He felt sorry for me, but he was too embarrassed to tell me straight out, and so he'd run off to help her and now was laughing about it to hide how he really felt... Or at least that's how I saw it. Anyway, asking me why I'd "messed her up" was *soooo* much cooler than just telling me to cheer up or something—the kind of thing other people would have said. And it had been *waaaay* better just to leave me at the nurse's office like that. *Waaay.*

Still, it did sound a little like he was more worried about Maki than me, so as he was taking off his shoes in the doorway I kicked him—my patented Aiko whip kick, a roundhouse to the upper body that I learned from my brother. My bare foot struck his arm—*chiban!*—and he bent double, letting out a little yelp. Humpf. Drop dead. No, on second thought that might cause trouble.

"Thug," he muttered.

"You deserved it."

"Dear God, please grant me the patience to teach the ways of peace and nonviolence to this foolish, violent girl."

"Say your prayers, you lousy monk. Didn't you hear? God is dead."

"Where'd you learn to kick like that?"

"My brother taught me."

"Figures. Anyway, are your mom and dad around?"

"No…"

"Then let's go!"

"Okay, but why not come in for a minute?"

"No, I think we should go out."

"Okay, but what about Kita and Shiba and the others?"

"Gone."

So…he didn't want to come in because he was alone. Didn't want to be alone with me—when it would have been such a perfect chance. Perfect for me, anyway.

"Uhhh," I murmured.

"What?"

What? "There's something I need to get first. Come in for just a second."

"I'll just wait here," he said.

"But it may take a minute, even longer."

"No problem. Take your time."

"But we've got these great cookies you can eat while you wait."

"No thanks. Don't bother."

Ooooh, what a dummy. "Okay, hold on a minute," I said, and ran up the stairs to pretend to get something I had pretended to need. I stood at the top of the stairs, conscious of him waiting below at the door. He's here! In my house! What to do? What to do? This might be a once-in-a-lifetime opportunity. I had to get him up the stairs and, if possible, into my room. But how? I'd bought some time with the bit about needing to come up to get something. But how was I going to get him up here? And how was I going to get him to fall into my bed? I went into my room, plans spinning in my head, and closed the door behind me. Then I started picking up all the stuff I had flung everywhere. All those magazines, empty cans, half-empty bottles, shirts and sweatpants I'd stripped off and thrown on the bed—but holy crap! It would take forever to pick it all up. No good. I couldn't bring Yoji in here. Looks like today was a no-go. Maybe a love hotel?

I should have six thousand yen or so in my wallet—just about enough for a love hotel with the daytime discount. It would probably seem weird for the girl to pay for the room, but I was willing to do anything for Yoji.

Okay. I climbed out of my jeans and changed into some really pretty Triumph panties I'd just bought. And the matching bra. Quick check of the pits and pubs, adjust the eyebrows, comb through my hair, then back into the jeans and a shirt. Perfect. But…why was I so *totally* nervous? I guess because the idea of doing it with Yoji was suddenly getting real. I could tell I was already a little wet down there.

Wait a minute! Don't get ahead of yourself. Calm down, Aiko. Nothing was decided yet. Too soon for those love juices.

But try telling that to the juices. Did I need to change panties again?

No point really. And these were the cutest anyway.

I stuffed my wallet, cell phone, a mirror, and a hankie into my purse and slung it over my shoulder. Then I left my room and went back downstairs. No sign of Yoji. I put on my shoes and went outside. There he was—standing on the other side of the street by a telephone pole—not even looking this way.

I locked the door behind me and crossed the street to where he was standing. But in the few seconds it took me to get there, my heart started pounding and fluttering and bending all out of shape and just about jumping out of my chest. Scary stuff.

"Sorry I took so long," I managed to say.

"No worries. Is there a park somewhere around here?"

"Not exactly, but there's this little playground just down the street."

"Why don't we go there?"

We set off together, shoulder to shoulder. I couldn't believe I was walking along through my neighborhood with Yoji. It was like a dream. I could barely talk.

"What were you doing?" he asked suddenly.

What was I doing? I was changing my panties. "What was I doing when?" I said.

"Just now," he said. "You said you needed to get something?"

"I did? Uh, I've been thinking about a lot of stuff today, and I guess I'm a little dazed."

"Are you okay?" he asked. "You shouldn't let yourself get so worked up about everything."

"Everything?" I was only worked up about one thing.

"You know, Sano and Maki and everything."

Was he kidding? "I'm not worried about any of that." I really wasn't. Yoji was the only thing on my mind.

"Okay, forget it."

"Well, I suppose I was thinking about Sano being kidnapped."

"Who wouldn't be?"

"So," I said, "what do you think happened?"

"What do I think? I think somebody grabbed him and took him someplace. I've been trying to figure it out myself. Who'd have the motive?"

Motive? The only reason you kidnap somebody is for money. And there were lots of people who wanted money. In fact, just about all of us did—including me. Not an hour ago I'd been thinking I would cut off my own toe if the price were good enough.

I started to tell Yoji about my idea. How Sano had probably faked the whole thing himself. Yoji walked along beside me, listening but not saying anything. I was just explaining how he could have managed it when we got to the playground.

"Makes sense, doesn't it?" Yoji looked a little skeptical.

"Maybe," he said. "But a few things in your theory don't quite add up."

Huh? "Like what?"

"Well, for one thing, they said the toe had started to stink by the time his mother found it. That means it was cut off a while ago. Which also means it was too late to reattach it. If he'd been planning to have it sewn back on like you said, he would have put it on ice and had it delivered as fast as he could."

Now that he mentioned it, that did make sense. If I were going to part with my toe, even for just a little while, I wouldn't treat it like shit. I'd want to ice it up and wrap it carefully. Maybe even put it in a really pretty box and deliver it myself, leave it somewhere obvious so they'd be sure to find it right away, then ring the doorbell and run like hell. Would that be too much to ask for your own toe?

"And he would have been worried about how long it would take to collect the ransom. If he wanted to have the toe reattached, he would have been in a big hurry."

He had me there. Oh well.

"When you think about it, your theory doesn't make sense. And there's one other hole in it. It seems Sano's parents couldn't get their hands on anything like ten million yen. They look sort of rich, but they don't have that kind of money. They would have had to sell their house to get it. In that case Sano wouldn't have had anywhere to come home to after getting the ransom, and he knew that."

"I see what you mean, but how do you know all that stuff?" I asked.

"Know all what stuff?" Yoji said.

"That the Sanos didn't have the money and all."

"It was on their website."

"Website?"

"You didn't know? Sano had his own website, and his mom and dad posted stuff about the kidnapping. Everybody was talking about it. Then they started this fundraiser to get the ransom money together. Said they would still need two million yen more after they'd sold off everything they owned, that they'd have to sell the house in three days' time if they couldn't raise the whole ten million. It's all there, right on their site."

"No way!" Some people have no self-respect. Then again, their son had been kidnapped. "So did they get the two million?"

"It doesn't look like it. I think everybody thought it was a joke." Who wouldn't? Something like that appearing all of a sudden on the web—looks kind of fishy.

"Then last night they added a link to Voice of Heaven, and everybody started posting on the bulletin board and it went totally viral. It was crazy. Apparently that was the end of his mom and dad's attempt to raise the money."

Of course it was. You can't put anything true on the web. You can't tell people what you really want—or need. You can't get your prayers answered by tossing them into some fictional universe.

Pretty pitiful. Sano's mom and dad…and their prayers.

Pretty pitiful to ask when you know ahead of time no one is going to answer.

"So they'll have to sell the house," I said.

"Don't say that—or at least don't make it sound so simple. Where would they go?"

"It doesn't matter how it sounds, they'll still have to sell the house. If you want to change the situation, you have to change how you deal with it, change the whole game."

"I suppose you're right. But that's why I want to find Sano before it comes to that. That would solve the problem."

"Yeah, I guess," I said. But it also sounded practically impossible. I mean, especially if Sano hadn't faked the whole thing—I mean if he really had been kidnapped, and a real kidnapper had cut off his toe and really sent it to his house and wanted real ransom money. That was truly scary. Totally creepy. No?

"You've got to stop sticking your nose into stuff you don't understand, Yoji. It might be dangerous."

"Don't worry," he said. "I'm not alone. There are a bunch of us."

"Then you should leave it to the bunch. Why don't we forget about it for now and do something else?"

"Don't be ridiculous!" he said.

Why did everybody care so much what happened to Sano? Were he and Yoji really such good friends?

"I didn't think you and Sano hung out together," I said, sitting down on some sort of playground ride that looked like a pink bear stuck on a spring. The bear tipped over, and I went with it.

"That has nothing to do with it," Yoji said. "If somebody's hurting right in front of you and you can do something to help, you do it. I don't get worked up about trying to save refugees in Ethiopia, but when some guy in our class has been kidnapped, then I can't help worrying—and trying to do something. Who wouldn't?"

You're right, Yoji. Not many people would say it out loud, but you're right: sympathy has limits and borders. Even if somebody is really hurting, writhing in pain, if the pain is happening far away, or if it somehow doesn't seem real, then almost nobody would take the trouble to lend a hand or walk across the street or even so much as glance sideways. That's natural enough—just the way things are—but no one is willing to admit it. The urge to help and to stay out of it always seem to be at odds somehow.

I suppose people can only do what they want to do.

Or maybe that's not right. I wanted a Yoji who was some kind of hero, who was willing to help anybody, not just Nizaki or Urayasu or Sano from our class, but the refugees in Ethiopia or the man in the moon or aliens lost in some wormhole.

But there was nobody like that, and it might be scary if there were. A guy like that would have to spend all his time trying to preserve his hero image. So I guess I'd rather have an honest, forthright Yoji. He's cuter that way anyway.

Still, even if it was just to preserve his image, it might be nice if he wanted to help Ethiopian refugees or the man in the moon or aliens from another dimension. I think I would like a guy like that. Everybody's got a self-image to protect.

Still, it's probably best to leave the refugees and the aliens and the man in the moon to a real hero. The rest of us—Yoji and me and everybody else—we have a lot of other stuff on our plates, like real life. With all that to keep us busy, our sympathy for others and our desire for them to fuck off end up tugging us in opposite directions. I'm always like, "Pooor baby!" and then the next minute like, "Dumb asshole!" But then who isn't?

But I really do want Yoji to turn out to be a hero. I want his compassion, his "poor baby," to win out over his "dumb asshole." And if he went running off to Ethiopia or the moon or another space-time dimension, well, I'd go right along with him.

No, what am I saying? I totally love Yoji just the way he is.

And he was sitting next to me right now, not saying anything, just swaying back and forth on the neck of a springy giraffe. The paint was peeling and the yellow spots looked even spottier. I was pretty sure he must be feeling a little embarrassed right now, thinking he'd been too honest, that he'd said some stuff he didn't need to say. He probably couldn't figure out what to say next, not until I spoke up. So he just sat there—bounced there—watching me and looking a little sheepish.

I should really say something, I thought.

On the other hand, why bother?

So there it was: the tug-of-war between care and not care.

Shit! My heart was pretty puny. It looked like my urge to avoid trouble was going to win out, even with a guy I really liked. But that was wrong. Just plain wrong!

So…

"So, Yoji." Was that what I should say? "Do you think you can find Sano?" How was that?

"No way of telling," he said. "But there's been no trace of him since that night. Looks like you were the last one to see him."

"Somebody's hiding something."

"Could be," he said.

I was the last one to see him. What of it? "So do you think I'm involved too?"

"Me? No, of course not! Why would you want to kidnap Sano?"

"You're right, why would I?"

"That's what I said. So why would I suspect you?"

"So why don't you stop saying that I was the last one to see him?"

"That doesn't mean anything. It's just a fact. Nobody's making any more of it than that."

"Fine, then drop it. I don't want to hear any more about it."

"Fine. But there's something I want to ask you, if you don't mind."

"What?"

"Do you think there might be some guy who likes you?"

I played dumb. But I felt like somebody had punched me in the back of the head. "What are you talking about?" I held my breath.

"I was just thinking that a guy who liked you would be pretty mad that you and Sano went to a love hotel together, and that he might be the one who kidnapped Sano. It seems like a possibility. Of course, I could be all wrong."

"What are you talking about? You've got to be kidding me."

"Why do you say that? It's not impossible."

"It's *totally* impossible. Because there isn't some guy who likes me."

"How can you be so sure? It might be some guy you don't even know."

"A guy I don't know...?" You asshole! Drop dead. Right now, Yoji, drop dead! Disappear. Dissolve. Become nothing. Every last trace of your mortal existence.

"I guess it was a dumb idea."

If it was a dumb idea, then apologize.

"Sorry," he said. Then he looked away, and as I glanced at his profile I knew that my cute Triumph bra and panties were not going to be making their debut anytime soon. And I'd gone to all that trouble to change, and they were *really* cute. Oh well. I didn't even want to have sex with Yoji anymore. Not really. Probably not anyway. Whatever. I just wanted him to leave. To disappear. How totally annoying. It was all so pointless. Pointless, pointless, pointless! Really for *real*, Yoji, just fuck off and DIE!

I wanted to get up and leave, but at the same time I was terrified he would just say "bye" and let me go. So I couldn't move. I also couldn't bear to look at him anymore. I wanted to ask him how he could sit there with that blank look on his face knowing that Sano and I had been to a love hotel, how he could ask me all those stupid questions about other guys who might like me. I knew how: he didn't care about me *at all*. I felt paralyzed sitting there next to him, felt pathetic as hell.

Shit, I was *not* going to cry. I was starting to cry. Oh, oh, oh, my eyes were burning. I clenched my teeth and looked down at the ground under the weird, pink rocking-bear. But when I squinted, it felt like the tears were going to start. I couldn't breathe. One false move and the dam would burst. My heart was beating like crazy. Shit, I could practically hear it! My temples started pounding, and all of a sudden there they were: major tears. I was looking at the ground, so my hair was probably giving me some camouflage, but that wouldn't work for long. He'd figure out what was going on pretty quick. Maybe I should run home. But somehow the short distance to the house suddenly seemed really *far*. Especially since I was frozen, unable to stand up or walk two steps. The last thing I wanted was for Yoji to hear me sniffling and sobbing. Yet I could tell if I moved even the tiniest muscle, I'd start bawling out loud. Totally embarrassing.

I willed myself to sit perfectly still or risk humiliation.

Shit! SHIT! It wasn't going to work! I couldn't stand it. I *was* going to cry. And it was going to be one honking flood of tears. Why not? I was *really* sad. I *wanted* to cry. Embarrassing or not, it didn't really matter anymore. I could feel the sobs and the sniffles and the snot working their way up my throat, marching up like they were about to attack. My hands were numb from being balled up so tight.

And then, just as I was thinking, shit, shit, shit, shit, shit, this is *it*…just as I was about to lose it, Yoji stood up as if he was about to walk away.

"I don't believe it," he murmured. Was that lucky timing, or what? Or *what*? In one blast, I breathed…out everything I had been holding inside, then took a few gulping gasps and—then I lost it.

"*Hiii…ku, fu, eeeee, ggu, fuu…*" I couldn't believe how pathetic I sounded—couldn't believe this was coming from my own mouth.

And getting louder every second. It was out of control. I wanted to cry, and that's what I was doing. What was wrong with that? I wanted somebody to tell me that it was okay for anybody as sad as I was to cry her eyes out for as long as she wanted. But then just as all my blubbering and yelping was about to jack up to some new and more disgusting level, I noticed, out of the corner of my eye, that Yoji was standing a little ways off…talking to someone? "What do you think you're doing?" he was saying.

You idiot! Yoji! You asshole! I'm bawling my eyes out here and you don't even *notice*. Asshole! Drop dead! Do you hear me, Yoji? DROP DEAD!

"You can't do that here," he was saying, his voice getting really stern. "Don't you know where you are? I'm calling the police." This made me look up. I didn't even care if he saw me like this. And anyway, if I didn't look up he'd never realize I was crying.

But did I get a shock—enough to stop me mid-sob, like I was sucking back the tears, which had mostly been for show anyway.

Because now I saw why Yoji sounded so mad: he was standing in front of a couple who were on a bench next to the swings, no more than a few yards away. The man's pants were down around his ankles and the woman's skirt was tucked up to her waist, and they were going at it, right there. No doubt about it, they were doing it. They were bumping uglies, and they didn't seem to care who saw, much less that Yoji was pissed off. There they were, in broad daylight, on a park bench, almost fully clothed, fucking their brains out. But one look told you this wasn't some pervert thing they were doing—because the whole time they were going at it, the whole time he kept putting it in and taking it out and putting it in and grinding it all around, they were both crying their eyes out. And the tears had nothing to do with the ones I had just been shedding. They weren't working themselves up and making themselves cry to make a point about something, the way I had been. You could tell that these tears had come pouring out all by themselves. I could see the difference right away. Because my tears had been fake, and theirs were totally real. Maybe it was *because* I had just been crying fake tears that I knew the real thing when I saw them.

But shit! If they were doing it in broad daylight on a park bench, why were they *crying*, real tears or not? It *did* look kind of cool, kind of *out there*, to be doing it right in the open like that; but somehow I could tell there was nothing fake or showy about either the tears or the sex. They weren't exhibitionists—somehow I knew that right off the bat. They were crying because they couldn't stop from crying, and they were fucking because they couldn't keep from fucking. Of course they were. If they weren't, why did they go on doing it—crying and fucking—even when Yoji went right up and told them to stop?

I gave a little rub to my cheeks—but the fake tears had dried in no time.

"I said *cut it out!*" Yoji said, whipping out his cell phone. "I'm really going to call the cops." I hauled myself up off the pink bear and went over to him.

By this time, the guy had started moaning, but the woman looked up and murmured, "Go ahead, call them. Do whatever you want. It doesn't matter." We could see everything now, the skin and pubs rubbing together between the rolled-up skirt and the pulled-down pants, and hear the sound—*gucha gucha, chappo chappo*. There was something so sad about it that I started feeling miserable again, but in a whole different way.

"I'm not kidding," Yoji said, starting to punch buttons on his phone. "I'm really calling them." So I reached around from behind and grabbed it out of his hand.

"Hey!" he shouted. "Give it back, Katsura. This is disgusting. What if some kids were to walk by?" But I didn't give it back. Instead, I just stood there, looking at their crying faces and their plastered-together parts. "Give it back," he repeated.

I knew who they were: Takaaki and Sayaka Yoshiba. They'd had three sons, triplets named Shin'ichi, Koji, and Yuzo, and all three boys had been killed by someone who called himself the Round-and-Round Devil. The bodies had been completely dismembered—arms, legs, and heads cut off—and the pieces had been left along the banks of the Tama River. The Round-and-Round Devil was still at large.

So even if this didn't exactly give them the right to sit on a park bench bawling—and balling—it seemed only fair, to me anyway, that we should let them go at it, at least for a while longer. These were *real* tears, and if they couldn't stop themselves from fucking while they were crying them, then so be it. At least that's the way I felt about it.

And they did seem pretty much determined to keep at it for the time being, but just as Yoji was about to interrupt them again, things got even weirder. A guy appeared out of nowhere, ran up to the bench, stared down at the couple, did this dramatic kind of double take—"Whooooa"—and stood there with this bizarre look on his face. But it wasn't just his look that was weird—it was everything about him. He was wearing a pink polo shirt tucked into chinos. A little Hello Kitty doll hung off his backpack. He was pale as a ghost and wore these big glasses that were almost covered by long bangs. And he had on this *really* weird hat. The whole effect was gross—like that disgusting guy on TV, Bondo

Oki. I was beginning to think it was something about this park.

But almost as soon as he appeared, the woman, who had seemed completely hot for it until that moment, suddenly pulled away from her husband and rolled down her skirt—I assumed she must know the weird guy somehow. And then the man, Mr. Yoshiba, began slowly pulling up his pants, though he still had a hard-on, and when he was decent again, he got up and walked away without saying a word.

But the Bondo guy was all squirmy and giggly. "Sorry," he said. "Did I interrupt something?" Then he turned to the woman, apologized again, and ran out of the park, his long hair and Hello Kitty doll bouncing all the way.

By this time Yoji and I were pretty freaked out, so we turned around and headed back ourselves.

WTF.

I remembered I had been crying, but I couldn't remember why anymore.

Why should I when the tears weren't even real?

6

The Yoshibas live right near me. You go a little north until you hit the Nogawa River, turn left and follow the bank for about five minutes, then down this little alley. It's right there. The whole place was crawling with media until just recently, clogging up the streets with cars and bikes and nosy neighbors and gawkers. It was a regular madhouse. But that was over now. It'd been more than two months since the Round-and-Round Devil kidnapped little Shin'ichi, Koji, and Yuzo, cut them up, and dumped them

in a heap by the river. Since then, a slasher in Nigata Prefecture
had run through a shopping center stabbing everyone in sight.
He managed to kill seven people and wound five more before
heading for the hills. Everybody was really tense for a week or
so until they found his body—he had committed suicide. And
then there were the three families living tooth-to-jowl in Tottori
Prefecture. A three-way feud that had been simmering for more
than a decade boiled over one night. Weapons of choice: kitchen
knives, hatchets, aluminum bats, lead pipes. Casualty count: four
dead, twelve seriously injured. Afterwards, there was an even
bigger stink in the village when they found out that the whole
thing had been stirred up by a woman who wasn't even related to
any of the three families. She took off out of the village, and the
media followed her with helicopters and everything, and in the
end just about everybody in Japan was watching the chase on live
TV—and nobody even seemed to remember the mass murderer
in our neighborhood anymore.

But to get back to my story, in the two years leading up to
the Round-and-Round Devil killing the boys, he had apparently
killed seven cats and four dogs—maybe more—and left notes by
the bodies, labeling them "Souvenirs of a Visit from the Round-
and-Round Devil." There were even little pictures with some of
them—supposedly drawn by the Monster himself. I'm not sure
what they showed, but they said they were these weird whirlpool
shapes. Shit, it was all just copycat stuff, riffing off those notes
about the "Bamoidoki God" left by that Sakakibara kid who cut
off that little boy's head, or that other killer who called himself the
"Jawakutora God."

You shouldn't go stealing other people's gods.

But then isn't all religion a matter of stealing in the first place?
The "religious spirit"—a big rip-off?

It's all about losers, big zeros who suddenly panic and figure they've got to find something to go nuts over, so they look around everywhere and they see other losers praying their guts out to the sky or a cross or some statue, and they figure "Shit! *That* looks good" and they end up doing the same thing—that's all religion is, deep down. Then there's missionary work—spreading the Good News—which is even worse. You go out and find other frustrated, pathetic fuckers and sell them the same crap, tell them to pray to the same whatever until they're dead. But you know, I don't really give a shit what people do—fool each other, copy each other, even help each other; as long as they don't bug other people, it's all good with me. But when it comes to these really pathetic bastards who use a bogus religion or their "principles" or "ideology" as an excuse to kill cats or dogs or little kids—well they can just fuck off and die.

So as for the creep who calls himself the Round-and-Round Devil…well, you pretty much know what he can do.

The little notes he left—those were totally like his calling card: like, "Round-and-Round Devil man was here!" But what the hell were those stupid whirlpool drawings? Self-fucking-portraits? So then maybe he isn't even human. But of course he's human, so what we've really got is a killer who is some sort of immature child, completely fucked up in the head and unable to tell the difference between this bogus Round-and-Round Devil god and the (human) idiot who made him up and worships him—an idiot who can't tell the difference between subject and object.

Or maybe just a kid.

These days it always turns out to be kids who do really wacked-out shit. Almost like it's some kind of fad. Come to think of it, killers do seem to be pretty fashion conscious, in their own way. When they're thinking of murdering somebody, I bet they go through all the possible ways and think, Well, *that's* totally last week, or That's definitely trending, or That's going to be all the rage this fall. They need a fashion sense to sniff out the season's coolest way to kill.

My brother told me that in the old days murderers didn't usually cut up bodies. In those days, when you cut up a body it was because you wanted a lot of pieces to scatter around in places where a lot of people could see them. You didn't cut up a body with the idea of keeping the murder a secret. But then someone discovered that cutting up a body made it easier to carry it away and bury it, and then a lot of people caught on and everybody started doing it. A fad, in other words.

Now you've got all these morons with their made-up gods—of course *all* gods are made up—and murdering children in their name in totally gross ways, and it doesn't look like that fad is going away anytime soon. It's starting to get annoying. All these sick fucks who kill for their god. And just because the killers happen to be kids this time, that doesn't mean it's going to make it seem all new and fresh, at least not for long it isn't. In fact, I'm way over them already. Drop dead, you fuckers. Who gives a fuck about you *or* your little monster gods? And anybody who thinks they're cute or funny or interesting can go to hell right along with them, right now.

And I'm not the only one who feels this way. That "Voice of Heaven" group that formed during the Sakakibara bullshit has been trying to find out who the Round-and-Round Devil is and get someone to kill him. As soon as the news came out, they started a campaign on their blog to "Flush the Round-and-Round Turd Down the Toilet." They even collected signatures of supporters and a whole lot of money for a legal defense fund for any hero who managed to off the asshole. Pretty cool. I hope someone *does* flush the Round-and-Round Turd straight down the crapper, and soon. I mean it, because just about *everybody* is sick as hell of his bullshit self.

Yoji and I were walking back from the playground, and I was thinking about all this stuff, thinking how these mass-murderer assholes *never* gave up. Then Yoji interrupted to tell me the latest.

"Did you hear that those Voice of Heaven guys have been middling in Chofu?"

"Middling?"

"It means 'grab every middle school kid you see and beat the hell out of him.'"

"You're kidding."

"They're convinced the Round-and-Round Devil is a middle school kid, and they say they want to smoke him out, like you smoke an animal out of its hole."

"I don't get it."

"It's a threat—they're telling the middle school kids that if they don't find out which one of them is the Round-and-Round Devil and hand him over soon, they're all going to get it."

"But how do they know for sure he's in middle school?"

"They don't. But they don't care. That's the way Voice of Heaven operates. They jump to conclusions and then run with them."

"You're serious?"

"Unfortunately, yes. The ones doing the beating are these big airhead V of H bruisers, egged on by the little scrawny computer geeks who've never been in a fight in their lives. But the ones getting the crap beat out of them are just regular middle school kids. I bet they have no idea what hit them. Think how they must feel when suddenly, out of the blue, somebody starts pounding on them. And it's happening all over Chofu."

"For real?" I said.

"For real," said Yoji.

"But I suppose that's just the way of the world."

"Not my world. I don't think we should take it lying down."

"Maybe not, but what can we do about it?"

"Fight back—beat up anybody we meet who's been 'middling.'"

I guess I could see his point. But now that I'd seen the Yoshibas crying and doing it like that, I knew that fighting back wasn't always the answer. There was something to be said for just giving up, just saying fuck it and letting things slide for a while to see how they develop. Just maybe, doing nothing might turn out to be the best thing, might even be the thing that catches the Round-and-Round Devil. I suggested this to Yoji.

"Don't be an idiot, Katsura," he said. "We've got to do something. Those Voice of Heaven thugs are hurting people. They're too anxious to get results. They're pissed off, and even though they don't really know who they're pissed off *at* they just can't stand it, so they go around picking on whomever they choose, almost at random. But it's nothing but a diversion. And they'll never catch the Round-and-Round like that."

"You're right, I guess." There was, of course, something in what Yoji was saying. On the other hand, they were at least doing *something*, and I didn't feel like criticizing anybody who was actually trying to bring down the Monster. Let them give it a try, I thought, even if their method was full of shit. It was better than doing nothing. Though I did feel bad for the middle school kids who were getting beat up.

After that, we walked along for a while without saying much. I was feeling a little bad that the poor Yoshibas' consolation fuck had been interrupted back there. They didn't seem to have much of anything left, so why shouldn't they fuck their brains out? On the other hand, there was something screwy—if you'll pardon the pun—about doing it right there on the little playground. So maybe Yoji had been right to try to stop them. Or not? Which was really better *for them*? If it was me and I was really horny, then I guess I'd rather they let me go on and do it. But I had to admit, to an outside observer it sure looked like it hurt more than it helped—what with all that crying and all.

Yoji seemed to be more worried about some hypothetical kid who might show up at the park than about the Yoshibas, which is why he tried to stop them. And of course he was right. Still, he could have shown a little more consideration for the unhappy couple.

Though that's probably totally wrong. You can't do it right out in the open like that, cock and twat to the wind. Makes a bad impression on the minds of our youth. Not to mention any adult who happens by. I mean, who wouldn't be messed up by seeing something *that* sad? Two grown people, fucking their heads off and crying their eyes out.

Still, you had to feel sorry for them. Totally sad sex brought on by a totally sad situation—so why not at least let them finish?

Sure you should. But then another thought occurred to me: the Yoshibas had lost their kids under the grossest, most totally terrible circumstances, but maybe out of that horribleness some new kind of sex had been born. Almost like holding all that sadness in your arms and fucking the sadness itself. Sex born out of the death of children. I know it sounds bad when you put it like that, but *sex that makes use of pain.*

The human need for sex is as strong as the need for food—another idea I got from my brother, but I think so too. And sometimes that need wins out, even over the sadness of losing your kids. Maybe lust is so stubborn it can even find a way to take advantage of the death of three little boys, to make some amazing fucking.

Which is a totally shitty thought.

But then I guess the human sex drive is a pretty shitty thing.

Though I also guess that without it, none of us would even be here. Our very existence depends on that shitty sex drive.

Pretty nasty, when you think about it.

Which is not to say that the Yoshibas' sex was absolutely that kind of sex, but it pretty much looked that way to me.

Yoji and I talked about the Voice of Heaven for a while. Then, when we got to my house, we somehow just couldn't say goodbye.

Of course, I didn't want him to go—though part of me also wanted to get away from him. Still, there was more stuff I wanted to say before we went our separate ways.

And I'm not sure why, but Yoji seemed to be in no hurry to leave either. Maybe he was worried that seeing the Yoshibas had somehow traumatized me. Or maybe he wanted to find out whether there was a guy somewhere who liked me and would be jealous about Sano—though all that already seemed like ancient history now. Or maybe there was something else he wanted to say. Or maybe he didn't have anything to say but just wanted to hang around with me a little more...or not.

Yep. Or not. "Well then, I'll be seeing you," he said. "Are you coming to school tomorrow?"

"I don't know," I told him. "Are you?"

"Probably. I'm not sure I can do anything more about Sano."

"That was pretty amazing," I said, "seeing them fucking like that."

"What? Oh, yeah, amazing."

I wanted to have amazing sex with Yoji. Or not even amazing—just nice, plain sex. No face shots, no freaky acrobatics, just your ordinary missionary position, nice and slow, with a sweet little orgasm when we were both ready. But I couldn't really tell him that. Instead, I asked whether he wanted to come in. Maybe have some tea?

"No, I'd better be getting home," he said, giving a little wave and turning to go. But instead of heading toward the station, he turned and went back the way we'd just come.

"If you pass the playground again," I laughed, "check to see if they've come back for seconds."

"I doubt they'll come back," he said. "If they do, I'll call the police."

"You wouldn't."

"Why not? We can't just let them go on doing that on a playground. I feel sorry for them too, but…Anyway, see you later."

"Right, see you later."

I stood at the door, making no move to open it, and watched him go. I'd managed to get Yoji all the way to that door, with no parents or brother waiting inside, and still no sex. There was something truly pathetic about that—and at the same time not.

If we'd had sex after seeing the Yoshibas, would we have used their sex to make ours more intense? Would that have worked? Would our lust have been strong enough?

Maybe not. Maybe it would have been weak; maybe we would be repelled by the memory of what we'd seen. Or maybe I had it wrong. Maybe Yoji was scared off by the realization that we were so close to having sex. Maybe that's why he turned on his heel and ran off like that. Maybe I was afraid myself, and that's why I hadn't been clearer about trying to get him inside, into my bed.

No, that wasn't it. Who was I kidding? Yoji just wasn't interested in having sex with me.

Was that it?

That was it.

What could you expect, once he found out you'd done it with Sano? What is a guy like Yoji going to think about a girl who has casual sex with every guy she runs into? Is he going to want to do it with you? How stupid are you? What do you expect?

How stupid am I? Pretty stupid, I guess. I guess with Sano I just had the feeling I wanted to have sex with a boy, and it didn't much matter which one. Just like I always assumed all boys' things spring to attention when presented with any anonymous muff. But maybe it doesn't always work that way.

I realize now. Not every boy is right for every girl, and for boys too, not every girl is the right one. That's just the way it is. At least for some girls and some boys.

I'm pretty much one of those girls who gets horny and gives in to the urge, but I suspect Yoji's not like that. I was going to need some sort of strategy to get him in bed. Some sort of trick. A tactical advantage.

But at that moment I was just really disappointed. I stood there at the door, watching until he was out of sight. Then I went inside. Oh cruel, cruel world…and all that crap.

But what's so cruel about it? I'll tell you what. It was cruel that I hadn't been able to have sex with Yoji, and crueler still that I hadn't even been able to kiss him. But cruelest of all was the fact that I was the sort of girl who was always *always* thinking about fucking and kissing and nothing but fucking and kissing and everything that went with them. It was cruel to be me.

It was different for Yoji. That much was obvious.

Yoji was thinking about Sano. He was thinking about those kids who might stumble into that little park and catch the Yoshibas fucking. And he was thinking about the Yoshibas. Even the fact that he had forced them to stop showed that he was concerned about them. He didn't want them to get in trouble for what they were doing, didn't want other people to see them like that. That's what he was thinking about.

And you had to admire him for that. He's a noble soul.

And I'm an idiot. An idiot who never thinks about all the

things she should be thinking about.

But then again, what kinds of things have I got to think about? And what good would it do for me to think about them anyway? I don't understand much of anything.

But it would be even worse to give up and not think about anything at all. Just like you're expected to do the right thing even if there's a chance you're being hypocritical when you're doing it, so too you should try to *think* the right stuff even if you didn't really believe any of it. That's just the way things are, Aiko.

So I lay down on the sofa in the living room, fully intending to put my brain to work thinking about where Sano might be— but before I'd thought about it for more than five minutes, I was sound asleep.

Like I said, I'm pretty much an idiot.

7

So Kerstin was there in my dream, and I was there with her. We were two different people, but she looked exactly like me. We were out in this big grassy field next to the Tama River, looking for a soccer ball. It was starting to get dark and we still couldn't find it, and we began to notice that everybody else had gone home. We got more and more nervous. "Where's the ball? Where's the ball?" Like that. I felt like I was going to cry, but then I could see Kerstin off in the distance, just her silhouette, holding up her hand like she wanted to let me know she'd found it. But somehow I knew she hadn't. What she had found in the bushes was the bodies of the three little kids, all chopped up in pieces, and she was trying to lure me over so she could scare the hell out of me.

She waved again and again to get me to come, but I wouldn't budge. I was trying to figure out how far it was to the road from the spot where I was standing. If I sprinted, could I make it there and stop a car to get help before Kerstin caught me?

But when I looked back at the dark mass of the bushes, Kerstin had vanished. I looked around at the field, but there was no sign of her anywhere.

No, not vanished. She had hidden somewhere, and I was sure she was sneaking up on me. Probably with some part of one of the kids clutched in her hand.

I woke to find my brother perched on my back, bare legs sticking out of his shorts, reading the sports pages. My heart was pounding from the dream. "Get off," I muttered, my face pressed into the sofa, but he stiffened his legs and tried to keep me from shaking him off. The rest of his body is pretty scrawny, but thanks to years of soccer his legs are thick and muscly. It suddenly occurred to me that those heavy limbs pressing down on my back must have caused my nightmare. But was that really possible? Did dreams really work like that? Could I really have gotten the idea for the soccer ball in my dream from his legs, even while I was sound asleep? Not likely. That would take ESP or something.

Whatever.

Maybe he'd been talking while I was asleep; maybe I'd heard his voice and made the connection to soccer and then gone looking for the ball.

Whatever.

"What are you doing sleeping?" he said. "What's for dinner?"

"How should I know?" I said.

"Where's Mom?"

"She said she'd be working late tonight."

"Then why didn't you make dinner?"

"Because I was asleep," I told him.

"Which is why I asked what you were doing sleeping."

"I was tired. So I slept."

"What kind of an excuse is that?"

"No excuse. Just human nature. People sleep when they're tired. When they're not tired, they don't sleep."

"That's not what I meant…Awhh, forget it. Stop chattering and get cooking."

"I don't feel like it," I said. "You do it."

He didn't look happy about it, but he got off my back and shuffled out to the kitchen. I've got him pretty well trained. Fortunately.

"What're you going to make?" I called after him.

"What?" he called back. I could see him opening the lid on the rice cooker and peering inside. "Shit! You didn't even make any rice."

"Soooooorry!" I called back. Not that it was my job to make rice, but I didn't mind a little apologizing, seeing as how he was going to make dinner.

"How about pasta? I'm totally starved, and I'm not too good at making rice."

"Pasta's fine," I said.

My brother is a pretty good cook. He doesn't have much of a repertoire, but the few things he makes are tasty. Mom's a good cook too. She even went to cooking school way back when, and I guess my brother picked up some stuff just by watching her. He's a quick study. In fact, he's pretty quick at everything.

First, he peeled and crushed a knob of garlic. Then he seeded a hot chili and chopped it up fine, took some bacon out of the freezer and unwrapped it. Next he cut up an eggplant, dumped it in a dish, and put it in the microwave. After he'd finished chopping an onion, he put a frying pan on the stove, heated some olive oil, and tossed in the garlic. Next came the chili, the bacon, and the onion. When all that had been frying for a few minutes, he added the eggplant, which had been softening in the microwave, and cooked it some more. Finally, he opened a can of tomatoes, mashed them up, and added them to the pan. Salt, pepper, a few tablespoons of stock, a drizzle of soy sauce. And a pinch of sugar to finish it off. Then he turned off the heat and let the sauce cool. While it was cooling, he boiled a pot of water and put the pasta in. When it was just about done, he turned on the burner and reheated the sauce. After draining the pasta, he added it to the pan and warmed it all up. Voila!

As I lay there on the couch, I found myself following his progress with my nose. The smell of the oil heating in the pan, the fragrance of frying garlic. And finally, the unmistakable smell of tomato sauce wafting in from the other room. It smelled good! In fact, I knew it *was* good, since he made this spaghetti a lot.

Whoa.

Just as my mouth was starting to water for real, the phone rang. *Brrring, brrring,* ring, ring, ring, ring.

"Telephone!" I called.

"You get it," he called back from the kitchen.

"I can't. I'm weak from hunger!"

"Don't be ridiculous," he shouted. "You're in there, you answer it." But as he said this he came into the living room. He really is well trained.

While he was answering the phone, I got up and went into the kitchen. I got out some plates and began serving the pasta. This was a job I could manage.

Up close and personal, the pasta smelled even more delicious. And *really* garlicky. Not that I objected. It really *was* mouthwatering, and my mouth really *was* watering. A man should know how to cook. As I was dividing up the pasta between two plates, I started hearing what my brother was saying in the other room.

"Really? Are you serious?"

Serious about what?

"That's terrible," he was saying. "Is she okay?"

Is who okay? Mom? Had something happened?

No, it couldn't be Mom. If something had happened to her he wouldn't be standing there asking if the guy on the other end of the phone was "serious."

Then who? Or what?

"Don't do anything stupid," he said. "Try to keep everybody calm. Okay, right. I know, but…okay. But that's where you're wrong. They've got nothing to do with it, really…Don't say stuff like that. Don't talk about who's going to take responsibility. Nobody's really responsible in a case like this…I know, but you don't really know what's going on, so don't get all excited. Wait till we know more about it. We can figure it out later…For now, just let it slide. Wait a bit…"

The line seemed to go dead, and my brother stood for a moment staring at the receiver in his hand. Then he set it back in its cradle.

"Idiots," he muttered.

Who or what?

"What?" I said.

"What? Oh, nothing."

"Who was that?"

"A friend."

"Did something happen? To Mom?"

"What? Oh, no, not that kind of friend. It was about the Yoshibas. You know, the people who had all that trouble. The Round-and-Round Devil."

"I know, but what happened? What's up now?"

"It only gets worse. Mr. Yoshiba just committed suicide."

"No, that can't be right."

"I'm afraid it's true."

"It's *not*. I just saw him."

"Saw who?"

"Mr. Yoshiba."

"Really? Where? Why?"

"I went to the playground today, and he was there."

"Alone?"

"No, I went with a friend."

"Not *you*, Mr. Yoshiba. Was he alone?"

"Oh, no, he was with his wife."

"Really? But how did they seem?"

"What? What do you mean, how did they seem?" Shit! They were fucking their brains out, right there on the bench, but I could hardly tell my brother that.

"What time were you there?"

"In the park?"

"Yeah, in the park."

"A little after three, I guess."

"Three?"

"But you're serious? Mr. Yoshiba really killed himself?"

"It looks that way. They said he hanged himself in their bedroom."

But how could he have? He must have gone straight home. Could he really be dead?

"I don't get it," I said.

I didn't. And I'd lost my appetite too. No way I could eat pasta now.

Or at least that's how I felt at that moment—a natural enough reaction. But in the end, I ate, and it was delicious. I was thinking about all sorts of stuff while I ate, so I can't say I enjoyed it as much as I usually did, but I still managed to put away a big plateful, *zuru zuru musha musha*! Yum. My brother ate his too. Neither of us said much, but the TV was on so it wasn't dead quiet.

When we were finished, we changed the channel to our favorite comedy show, *Downtown*, but we didn't feel much like laughing. Natural enough. I'm not sure how other people react to stuff like this, but I guess I found out that hunger trumps sympathy, for me at least, but they both trump laughter. You could write it like this: hunger > sympathy > laughter. My brother's phone never stopped ringing the whole time "Downtown" was on, but it was all texts. Every time one came in, he tapped out an answer, but almost before he could hit SEND, another one arrived, interrupting his answer.

During a commercial, I asked him what all the texts were about. He said they were about "nothing," but I knew that wasn't quite true.

Then the show came back on and I got up to go to the bathroom, but when I got back to the living room, he had vanished. I heard a noise from the front hall and went out to find him putting on his shoes.

"Where are you going?"

"Out," he said.

"Out where?"

"To see a friend."

"Why?"

"Why what?"

"Why are you going out? Did something happen?"

"No, nothing in particular."

"Stop fucking around and tell me *what's going on*!" I told him.

"Stop making a scene. Just let it go."

"I won't," I said. "I'm worried. If you won't tell me where you're going, I'll follow you."

"There's nothing to be worried about."

"It's a little late to be saying that now. You can't tell me it's nothing."

"That's exactly what I'm telling you."

"Okay, then you won't mind if I come along. In fact, I'm not even asking, I'm just coming."

"No, you should stay here."

"Then you've got to tell me what's going on."

"Okay, okay. The truth is, my friends are in a bit of a jam."

"What kind of a jam?"

"Those guys who called before were way crazy. Something really weird has happened."

"'Guys'? How many friends are we talking about?"

"Well, more than one."

"And they're all friends of yours?"

"Not all of them."

"And what was this weird thing that happened? What did you mean about 'taking responsibility'? Responsibility for what?"

"You don't miss a thing, do you? You know that Voice of Heaven blog?"

"Who doesn't?"

"Do you follow it?"

"Sometimes."

"Well, you shouldn't. But anyway, there's been a thread there about catching the Round-and-Round Devil."

"I know, I've seen it."

"Then you know about the guys who are beating up middle school kids thinking they'll catch the monster that way?"

"I've heard about it. But what? Are those guys your friends?"

"No, no. We've been trying to stop them."

"What? What are you talking about?"

"There are sort of two teams in Chofu right now: the guys who are 'middling,' beating up middle school kids, and some other guys who have gone to war with them to stop the beatings. My friends are in the second group. But the first group has been writing about Mr. Yoshiba's suicide on Voice of Heaven, stirring up trouble, and now they're out beating up kids all over town. So my friends have gone out to try to stop them, and the whole thing is getting out of hand."

Unbelievably dumb.

"Don't tell me you're going out to join them."

"No, I'm just going to try to stop them."

"You'll get sucked in."

"Don't worry, I won't let that happen."

"Like shit you won't. If you go out now, you'll have to pick sides."

"I won't. I won't get into the fight. But it's none of your business anyway. I won't be gone long. You just stay here."

"No, you need to stay here too. You can't go."

"Don't worry. I'm just going to get my guys to calm down, get them off the streets. I'll be right back."

"Okay, then I'm going with you."

"No you aren't."

"Yes, I am," I said, taking a step toward the door. But at that moment he bent down, picked up my shoes, and tossed them over my head into the living room. "Shit!" I said, turning around.

"I told you to stay here! I'll be back soon. But in the meantime I don't want you going out. It's not safe."

With that, he opened the door and ran out. By the time I got back to the hall with my shoes, he had disappeared out the door.

Idiot. Just like the other one standing here holding her shoes.

8

Some of the assholes who posted anonymously on Voice of Heaven had usernames like "God" and "Angel" and "The Holy Ghost." But now "God" and "Angel" and "The Holy Ghost" and all the others had gotten together in Chofu and were anonymously beating up middle school kids. They'd been talking for a while now about the "coming Armageddon." Was this what they meant? I turned on the computer and connected to the Internet, and as soon as I arrived at V of H I found a thread called "Armageddon in Chofu, Fall 2003," with live posts from both sides being added while I watched:

```
<Bagged three middlers. Kids these days have too much
 pocket money, so relieved them of 20K.>
 <Fight these fools! Middle school kids, strike back
  at the oppressors!>
  <In your dreams, dumbfuck middlers. The Seven Angels
   are coming!>
   <Don't take their money! The shit hits the fan
    if we get their parents after us.>
   <Bit late to worry about that now.>


<Now is the hour of curses and plagues! Our friend has
 died, but know this, you evildoers, a terrible death
 is stalking you.>
 <My mom was beaten up near Parco. She has nothing to
  do with any of this. You people are not human!>
  <You're right about that! We're GODS!>
   <Angels!>
    <Immoral seraphim!>
```

<You're fucking pubic hair!>

  <I'll take some of that pubic hair action! Yum,
  yum! Sticks in your teeth!>

  <Fucking otaku scum! Eat pubic hair and die!>

<Shit! They were making a break for it, but I got them.
They're at my place now. I got their skirts up and
they're not wearing panties. Looks like somebody
already got to them. Why should I want to keep this
tainted stuff around?>

<We're just hunting them, not breeding.>

  <Why not? Breed *on*, my man!>

<I thought this was a joke, but there's a *war* going on
in front of the Cultural Center. The God of the web
walks among us! This truly is the Voice of Heaven.
A buddy of mine waded into the battle and got the shit
kicked out of him. Better to let sleeping dogs lie,
I always say.>

<Served him right. Tell him to write a hundred
million pages about what happened and post them here
by tomorrow. Or else.>

  <Shit! Wish I were there! My blood's boiling. Sounds
  like things are *happening* on the Keio Line. I've got
  a homemade club and I am *ready* to go!>

  <Are you as stupid as you sound? If you get on the
  train with a club in your hand, the cops'll have
  your ass in a second, dickhead!>

  <You mean we can use our dicks? Mine's homemade
  too and ready to go!>

  <If you get on the train with your dick in your

hand, the cops'll have you just as fast.>
<But it's such a nice, "natural" weapon.>
<Don't think mine's long enough to do the job.
No beating with this thing.>
  <Make one yourself!>
<Take a taxi!>
 <What are you? A cabdriver?>
  <What? Have you got a laptop open on the
  passenger seat?>

<Just got back from the Cultural Center. Fight's over
and everybody has cleared out. But there was some
blood on the ground. Gyaaaaaaa!>
<Not sure what's going on. Trying to find out.>
 <What's going on? We're beating up middlers! Who
 is that?>
  <I live in Hokkaido and I'm in elementary school.
  If you want to hunt, you should come here.>
   <I'm at the airport and just bought a ticket for
   Hokkaido. My club's in my luggage!>
    <Hokkaido's a big place. Good luck, asshole!>
<The cops are massing at the station. Run for it,
Gods! Don't let them get you.>
<Middle school kids! Kick for the pricks! It's their
weakest spot! Happy dick-hunting!>
<Awh, don't pick on the poor little gods.>
 <Or make fun of their little dicks!>
  <OUCH!>
   <Kicked dicks!>
    <For a mere hundred million yen we can get that
    little dick up and running again for you.>

<A buddy of mine went out to have a look and they arrested him even though he had nothing to do with this. Poor bastard.>
  <Kiss the poor bastard for me.>
  <Shiiiiit!>

<I decided to breed little lamb after all, now that I've got her. And she gives awesome head.>
  <You people aren't human.>
    <Post your address. I want some too.>
    <Yeah, your address. How 'bout I fuck you with my club?>

<We've found the devil!>

<Stupid shits! If you find these little middle school punks, don't run over them. This is serious. The highway is a madhouse. No joke.>
  <He's right, I saw it too. Some girl with her leg crushed. Chofu is a war zone, and you can't tell who's in charge—God or the Devil or Yukito Ayatsuji!>
    <Who the fuck is Yukito Ayatsuji?>
    <No joke, somebody really is running down middle schoolers. Ha ha ha!>

<One of those middle school fuckers just stabbed me. Kill them all! Shit! Where's the hospital?>
  <My buddy was stabbed by a middle schooler and he's sitting next to me crying his fucking eyes out.>
    <A man lives and dies by his fists not knives.>

<Just gang-raped this little lamb. Left her near
Tamagawa Station.>
<You guys are gods! Or else fucking devils!>
  <One vote for devils.>
  <Make that two.>
  <Make it three.>
<Give those little shitheads a cigar!>
  <Three fucking cigars!>
    <One little, two little, three little shitheads.>
      <Shitheads, shitheads, shitheads!>
        <Enough already with the shitheads.>

<Went out to look around and the cops were all over
me like flies on shit. Asked a bunch of questions and
then beat me up for giving smart answers.>
<Nobody at the Cultural Center, but lots of blood.
 I'm scared shitless.>
  <Get a fucking clue! A girl was really raped at
  Tamagawa Station. Cops everywhere. The assholes who
  did this should go straight to jail.>
    <Who are you to judge?>
      <Are the riot police there yet? Because there's a
      riot in Chofu now.>
        <Not a riot, a fucking festival!>
          <No, this is Armageddon!!>

Sirens were wailing in the distance. It had actually started.
They'd been joking about another Armageddon, and this seemed
to be it. Three people had died in the last Armageddon, seven
in the one before that. Armageddon should be the final battle,

but this seemed to be happening over and over, an all-out riot—
and this one right here in Chofu. And it's pretty safe to say that
somebody's going to die. If it was just a bunch of middle and
high school kids fooling around, there wouldn't have been much
to worry about, but once the Voice of Heaven got involved, began
putting it out on the web, it was bound to turn into Armageddon.
Then every biker and punk from all over the area descended on
Chofu, and even the yakuza took advantage of the confusion and
came wading in. They pretended to come as peacemakers, but
they'd find lots of ways to turn a little Armageddon profit: beat
up on people and take their money; send some boys off to rape a
girl, videotape it, then blackmail all the parents—the rapists' and
the victim's—and then sell the video to milk the last bit of profit;
or maybe kidnap a kid, hold him a few days, and collect a little
ransom. There were lots of angles. The kids were looking for thrills,
thrills, thrills. But all the grown-ups wanted was money, money,
money. And then there were these guys who called themselves
"Street Angels," vigilantes who were supposedly trying to stop the
violence, got up in white T-shirts and black hats and carrying billy
clubs. On top of all that, the Voice of Heaven had come up with
an anti-anti-Armageddon squad of its own, which went to war
with the Street Angels—meaning that the "peacekeepers" were
doing everything they could to pump up the violence volume. The
only thing that might have helped would have been the untimely
death of the Temple of Johan guy who was in charge of the Voice
of Heaven, but no such luck.

But I suppose Voice of Heaven would have survived even if
Temple of Johan had died, and even if the site itself disappeared,
since there'd always be a new one to take its place. Armageddon
was an accident waiting to happen—over and over and over.

To tell the truth, up till now, when an Armageddon occurred, I pretty much just checked out, chalking it up to a bunch of assholes beating each other up. But when it happens in your own backyard, it's no joke.

About time you realized it.

You're right, it is about time. But that's just human nature. You don't really understand until it happens to you.

That may be so, but that's still no excuse.

You're telling me! I need to take a serious look at myself. And I'm going to, soon, going to totally clean up my act. But I had more than enough to worry about right now. My brother had gone out right into the middle of this craziness. As far as I could tell from checking Voice of Heaven, Armageddon was still happening all around the station. Our house is near the Nogawa River, a couple of kilometers away from the station in a ridiculously quiet neighborhood, so there was no reason to think that those idiot kids would bring their riot around here. Still, there was even less reason to assume that the kinds of assholes who fooled around on Voice of Heaven would act logically—if they were logical, why would we be in the middle of an Armageddon now? If they had one ounce of common sense, they wouldn't be following V of H in the first place. I was worried about my brother going off to join the mayhem, but there wasn't much I could do about it. He knew what he was getting into and decided to go anyway. Besides, he was a guy and also a fast runner—and I was pretty sure he didn't like to fight—so he would probably be okay.

Anyway, even if I was worried, it wasn't like I could go out looking for him. That would have been way too dangerous. Girls were getting raped out there. A lot of the stuff that was posted to V of H was bullshit, but I was pretty sure this was true. I was pretty sure some girl had been gang-raped and left for dead somewhere near Tamagawa Station—I don't know how I knew, but I just did.

It was dark out now, and something really creepy was stirring. The air felt heavy and warm, even though it was almost winter.

Or was I supposed to go out even though I didn't want to?

No!

Shit! I couldn't. It was scary out there. I had to stay here. No way I wanted to be chased by those assholes, beaten up, maybe worse. I didn't want to be in *Caged Fury*, but right now I was happy enough to stay put in my own little cage. Even if it meant getting in those lady fights with the beefy prison girls or the guards, it was still better than what was waiting out there in Chofu. That was some kind of bad shit. Fuck, it was Armageddon! But in my book they all had it coming—every one of those fuckers out there would die. My poor old peaceful Chofu, where you used to be able to go outside at night. Even to the playground...

Oh!

I suddenly remembered Yoji! Was he okay?

He had walked me home around four o'clock. It was almost seven now. Nearly three hours. He should be home by now. Yoji's house was just a few minutes from Tsutsujigaoka Station, so he should have just missed Armageddon in Chofu. I was hoping he was spending a quiet evening at home right about now.

But how would I know if I didn't check?

I picked up my phone and dialed his number. Riiiiiiing. Riiiiiing.

"Hello."

"Yoji? I'm glad I got you. What are you doing?"

"Not much of anything."

"Are you home?"

"What?"

"Sorry, I'm not checking up on you. I just wanted to be sure you were okay. Did you hear about the Armageddon in Chofu?"

"Yeah, I heard."

"So I was worried about you. I'm glad you're okay."

"Of course I'm okay. I'm always okay. You don't have to worry about me."

"I know, but I'm frightened. This Armageddon stuff is really scaring me."

"I know what you mean. Where are you now?"

"I'm home."

"Good, then stay there. It's just middle school and high school kids. They'll get worn out soon and head home. I'm sure it'll all be over by about ten."

"But I'm all alone!"

"What? Where are you parents?"

"Still at work. My brother was here, but he found out some of his friends were out there and he went to stop them."

"Playing hero, is he? But are you okay?"

What would you do if I said I wasn't?

"I'm scared, Yoji."

"You should call your brother and get him to come home."

My brother? I'm talking to you, you fool!

"Could you come, Yoji?"

Subtle, Aiko. Way to play it cool.

"I'd like to, but I'm kind of busy at the moment."

"Busy? Doing what?"

"Oh, you know, this and that."

"This and that? Until when?"

"Call your brother."

"He doesn't answer." Or he might not if I tried him. "Please come. I'm really scared."

"I can't right now."

"When can you?"

"Not tonight. I can't go out myself."

"Why not? Nothing's happening in Tsutsujigaoka. But it's a war zone here. You've got to come rescue me."

"I know you, Katsura. I'm sure you'll be all right."

Don't *say* that. I totally *won't* be all right. Who are you to tell me I will?

"I won't be all right. My brother's gone and I'm all alone."

I'd said it so many times now, I was beginning to convince myself. Don't cry, Aiko. You're not at your best crying. Shit! Why had I even called him?

"Chofu is really scary," I went on. "What am I going to do if somebody tries to get in?"

"Don't let them in." Duh!

"But what if they *force* their way in?"

"Then it won't make any difference whether you're in Chofu or Tsutsujigaoka or anywhere else."

"You mean it won't make any difference if I end up getting gang-raped and left for dead?"

What are you saying! Stop talking like that! You aren't even making sense. You just called to find out whether Yoji was safe at home. So why were you insisting now that he head straight for all the trouble in Chofu? How stupid and selfish can you get?

"Okay, okay," Yoji said at last. "Hold on. I'm actually in Chofu now. I'll come right over."

Really?

"Really? Where are you?"

"I just said, I'm in Chofu."

"But where in Chofu?"

"Right near your house."

"Really? Why? Are you back at the playground?"

"No! Why would I be there? Anyway, hold on, I'll be right over."

"But I don't understand. Where are you?"

"Like I said, I'm right nearby. I'll be over in a minute."

What the fuck? What the fuck? What the fuck? What was he doing in Chofu? Hadn't he ever gone home? Why was he hanging around here?

"Yoji, are you out banging with the Armageddon boys?"

"Don't be an idiot! I had something I had to do."

What a relief. I didn't want my Yoji mixed up with those Armageddon assholes.

"I'll see you in a second," he said.

"Yoji?"

"What?"

"Be careful."

"Don't worry, I will."

"No, I mean it. It's dangerous out there."

"Don't worry. I'll be right there."

Okay! He was coming here. For me.

For this very selfish girl.

"Okay, I'll be waiting."

"Okay."

"Hurry up."

"Okay, okay."

"And be careful."

"Don't worry."

"Okay, I'll be waiting."

Then the line went dead.

Maybe he was a little pissed at me?

But why was he still hanging around here? Where had he been and what had he been doing for the last few hours?

I checked V of H again. There were more than five thousand

posts to "Armageddon in Chofu." As far as I could tell, thirty or so middle and high school kids were going at it—maybe a little halfheartedly by now—down by the Tama River. Some of them apparently had lights. Fight Club after dark. When the cops came, they doused the flashlights, moved to a new spot, and started fighting all over. I wondered whether they would start jumping in the river like they did during the last Armageddon. Or throwing each other in. They lost two kids that way last time. The bodies still hadn't turned up.

As I sat there following all this in real time on the blog—or I suppose I should say, as I was sitting there with my head as empty as a bubble—it occurred to me that I should post something.

```
<Announcement from God. Aiko Katsura, who lives in
 Chofugaoka, in the city of Chofu, is the devil
 incarnate and a real toilet bowl. She's outside
 somewhere near her house, so get out and find her!
 Rape her! Kill her!>
```

I watched as my post appeared there in the stream, somewhere after the Fight Club in the dark business. Watched as "Aiko Katsura"—that's me!—was trailed by "devil incarnate" and "toilet bowl" and "Find her! Rape her! Kill her!" Why had I written that? I wasn't even sure I was the one who had. I knew my fingers had tapped out the words, but I had the feeling it wasn't really the "core" me moving them, not the me-within-me. But at the same time it did seem like the core me had done it, and the surface me simply hadn't realized what the deeper me was doing.

Whatever. The other users seemed to ignore my announcement. New posts kept coming up one after the other, and mine moved down the list, into the past. Maybe there was a mutual understanding, some natural code of ethics for this unethical bulletin board, that dictated that people ignore posts like mine, ones probably motivated by some sort of personal grudge rather than the desire to get the Round-and-Round. These guys may have been complete idiots, but they had some sense of decency, and the thing they hated most was anyone trying to manipulate them online.

But what kind of trouble had I been trying to stir up?

If Yoji was headed this way, why would I want to make sure the shit hit the fan just as he got here? Was I that desperate to see him? To turn him into a Yoji who had braved a town full of hoodlums to get to me? Was I upping the ante because I needed him to be an even bigger hero in my eyes?

Then I guess that made me the enemy of the heroes, a kind of antihero. I guess that made me the villain. And Yoji's enemy.

I guess that made me some kind of devil. I'm not sure, but I guess that post I wrote was the truth.

I really was a demon, and something of a toilet bowl.

Really, now that you mention it, I am a toilet bowl. A toilet bowl who had meaningless sex with Sano.

Shit!

No, no. I'm not a toilet bowl. Or a devil. No, I was pretty sure I had only done it with Sano because I loved Yoji, and that I was still punishing myself as a result. That's why I had called myself a devil and a toilet bowl on V of H. And pretending to be the voice of God was just another way of punishing myself.

But what if somebody saw that post and really did come after me? Maybe I had waded into deep shit. Was somebody really going to come after me, rape me, kill me?

And if they did, would that be a way of paying for what I'd done, making me clean again?

But how would that work? How would being beaten, raped, and killed make me pure again? Wasn't it just the opposite? Wouldn't that make me even dirtier? Make me even shittier? What the fuck was I thinking? What kind of dumbshit am I?

But just as I was going through all this again, my phone rang. Yoji? No. It was Kan. Fuck! Kan. Why was she calling me? I screwed up my courage and took the call.

"Hello?" "Aiko? It's me, Kan." "What do you want?" "Can you talk?" "Can I talk?" "Where are you?" "I'm home. Why do you ask?" I was suddenly on my guard. She probably wanted to get me outside and have another crack at the Crucifixion, but there was no way *that* was going to happen. Maybe she thought she could take advantage of the Armageddon confusion. Scary! No *way* I was going out now. But what she said next was completely unexpected. "It's really scary out there," she said. "Don't go out, no matter what. They're talking about you on the bulletin board. Somebody posted a threat, said they should go out and get you." Yeah, I knew. "Why?" I said. "I don't know, but somebody wrote on V of H that they wanted you caught and killed. They even said where you live. Does somebody have it in for you?" Does somebody have it in for me? That would be *you*, wouldn't it, Kan? After all, who had tried to crucify me? But before I pointed that out, what I really wanted to know was why she was telling me this. She wasn't my friend anymore, was she? "I don't think anybody we know did it," she continued, "but I'll call around and try to find out. Anyway, Aiko, don't go out. It's Armageddon out there." "Got it," I said. "I sent a request to have them delete the post about you, so I think it'll come down soon. In the meantime, is there someone there with you?" "No," I told her. "What? Where's your brother?" "He went out a while ago." "Not good! Try to get him on the phone and tell him to come home. It's really dangerous out there."

"Okay." "How about your mother and father?" "Still at work." "So, you're all alone?" "Like I said." "Do you mind if I come by?" she said. "Fine with me," I told her. Kan lived in Kichijoji, so it was a hike to Chofu. Plus she kept telling me how dangerous it was to be out now. Why did she want to come all the way here? Why? If she'd offered yesterday, when she was still my friend, I'd have told her to come right over. But what was this about now? What? Did she have another bone to pick with me? Was she trying to get me to drop my guard? Still, I knew she didn't write the post on V of H—because I wrote it myself! "I'll be there soon," she said. "No, don't bother," I said. "But if I take the bus, I can get to your house without going near Chofu Station." "But you said the post mentioned where I live, so it's not safe here. Don't come. I promise I'll stay inside and I won't move." I didn't mention that I was also hoping Yoji would be showing up. No need to go into too much detail. "I'll call my brother and tell him to come home, so you don't have to worry about me. But thanks." "Okay. But, Aiko, I wanted to say I'm sorry." "About what?" "About yesterday." "Oh that. Don't worry about it." I'd won anyway. "When I heard that Sano had been kidnapped, and then that his toe had shown up at his house, I guess I jumped to conclusions. I'm really sorry." "Like I said, don't worry about it. But I really didn't do anything to Sano." Other than kick him in the face. "I know," Kan said. "I know you didn't." "Okay." "I'm sorry, Aiko." "Okay, let's drop it." "Sorry, I…" she said, but then her voice seemed to dissolve in tears and I had a sudden flash. Kan actually *liked* Sano. I was pretty sure she'd done it with him too, but she wasn't one of the girls who'd told me I should give him a try. And somehow I had the feeling she'd always looked happy when he was around. That was it! That explained why she'd been acting so weird and emotional about the whole thing—why she still was. It was all part of a bigger picture. When Kan had seen the post I wrote on Voice of Heaven, she'd started thinking I would probably be killed. She must have wanted to apologize while there was still time. She had always been something of a goody-goody, or at least she liked to think so, so it would have bugged her if I'd gone and died before she could apologize for the attempted Crucifixion. That's what was behind all this. But who the hell cares? I began to relax as I listened to her sniffling and crying on the other end of the line. I knew I was just like her: we were both selfish bitches. And in the end I had no desire to punish her, no hard feelings at all. I'd have done just about anything to get Yoji to like me—just like Kan would have done anything to preserve her idea of herself as a kid who knew right from wrong, who would always try to make up for every mistake she made. Fine, that was fair enough. That's who you are—serious and all—and that's how you want to live your life. I've chosen the path of love instead…which suddenly reminded me that Yoji would be arriving any minute now, so I couldn't stay on the phone forever listening to Kan cry. "Stop crying," I told her. "It's okay. You don't have to worry about me. I'm fine. Thanks for calling, it's okay. I'm fine, so you can stop crying. Uhh, so, I'll see you at school, okay? Though I probably won't be going tomorrow. Text me. I'll get back to you. Okay? Thanks. Kan? Okay. I'll talk to you later. Of course! We're still friends. No, I *don't* hate you. Okay, talk to you later. Bye!" Whoa! If this love thing, if that's what it was, was going to make a girl like Kan do crazy shit like this, it was pretty scary.

But scary or not, it was the path I'd chosen, and I had to make the most of it.

Yoji would be here any moment. Or would he? I found it hard to believe he was really coming. Right through the middle of Armageddon.

I let myself imagine him, looking totally cool, dodging and weaving and avoiding all those people out there beating the shit out of each other, and coming straight here to me. It wasn't hard to picture, since all I had to do was remember how cool he'd looked when he'd come breezing in to rescue me from the bathroom.

The thread about Armageddon continued on Voice of Heaven, and my post was still scrolling down as more were added. When it finally disappeared below the bottom of the page, I felt myself relax a little and got a little more into my Yoji fantasy. But just then the doorbell rang. I put the fantasy on hold and went to answer it. "Coming, coming!" I called, just like some old lady—which was totally *not* what I wanted to sound like for Yoji. But when I pulled open the door, it wasn't Yoji standing there, or even my brother back from the wars. It was Maki, her bandage gone and her face as beautiful as ever.

She'd seen the post and was here already. That was fast.

Or not.

Maki lived in Edogawa Ward on the other side of the city.

But she'd heard about Armageddon and had come to take advantage of the confusion.

Scary.

And that would explain the hammer.

Part Two:
The Gate

The Cliffs

I'M SPRAWLED OUT on the sofa in our living room, listening. The sound of Armageddon keeps getting closer. At first I think I'm imagining things, but then I'm sure that those assholes from Chofu are headed this way, getting near our house. But then I hear something even worse: the screech of tires and a dull thud, like a bad car vs. pedestrian accident. But the tires squeal again and again, like the car is trying to get away. A hit-and-run? Then I hear it again: *gyrikikikikikigya! Dooooon!* Like another accident. But then I realize it's not an accident at all but just a car whacking into people one after the other. Hit-and-run, without the run. Vehicular middling? Middling homicide? Or maybe the counterattack had started—maybe this was the Revenge of the Middle School Kids. If it was, then I'm on it, hoppin' in the driver's seat, firing up the engine, grabbing the wheel, and smashing into the first God or Angel I see. *DOOON! Gyurugyuru DOOON! Gigiggkyu DOOON!* But as I imagined myself mowing down one person after another, the real car seemed to be getting closer. I could feel the air from outside, heavy with panic, slipping under the door. I could hear screams. "Whaaaaaaa!" *DOOOOON!* "Whoaaa! I'm serious! Cut it out!" *DOOOON!* "Gross! Stop!" *DOOOON!* More screams, footsteps running by outside. "Over there! Over there! Not there, look out!" "Kill him!" *Gyarigyarigyagyagyagya DOOON!* Then, right in front of my house, tires squealed, scattering gravel everywhere, and I could hear a crunching, like someone else being hit and thrown through the air. Then the shouts and screams and footsteps seemed to fade, as if everyone ran off. But just when I thought maybe the scary car had gone too, I heard the door creak open just outside and then slam shut. Someone had climbed out of the demonmobile and was standing right in front of my house. Scary. I was still lying there on the sofa, but I felt my body stiffen. What the what the what the? Then I could hear the driver's footsteps as he ran toward our door. Who could it be? I knew I should get up and run around turning out all the lights, pretend nobody was home, but I also knew it was already too late. The doorbell was ringing. *Chin-ton!* I froze. What the FUCK? But then I heard somebody calling my name. "Aiko!" What? It was my dad's voice! I jumped off the couch and ran to the hall. But when I opened the door, it turned out to be that weird old singer, Yuzo Gucci. But that was okay, I guess. A relief, really. "Are you okay, Aiko?" Yuzo Gucci said. Fine! Daddy? It was scary all alone. And my brother running off like that. What an idiot…I launched into the whole thing, standing there in the door talking to Gucci. But when I finally asked him to come on in, he told me it was dangerous to stay here and that I should come with him. Really? They weren't kidding about Armageddon.

But then Gucci had come in his car, and it looked like his bumper had taken care of a whole lot of those V of H guys on the way. Somehow, the sight of Yuzo Gucci's cute round face had a calming effect on my jangly nerves. He was tanned and relaxed and smiling, just like he was on TV. I told him to wait a minute and ran back to the dining room for a sweater I'd left hanging on a chair. Then I went back to the door, slipped into my shoes, and joined Gucci. Then I remembered the patio doors and told him I needed to go back and make sure they were locked. "Don't worry," he told me. "Nobody's going to try to get in if you're not in there to get." What? Did that mean they would have tried if I'd stayed there? I'm not sure I got it. But I knew it wasn't good. Gucci looked around as we left the house. It was cold outside. And dark. And suspiciously quiet, considering that it had sounded like a war was going on out here a minute ago. I felt like eyes were watching us from all different places around the house, and not friendly ones, eyes of people who would hurt us given half a chance. It looked like a million miles from our front door to anything that could be Gucci's car. From inside, it had sounded as though he had pulled right up on the front lawn, but now that we were out, I wasn't even sure which car was his. He told me to follow him, though, and we took off at a trot. I thought I glimpsed shady figures by the road, in the alley, behind the trees—but as we made our way down the street, there was no one to be seen. Had all the neighbors slipped off somewhere?

When we got near the raised banks of the Nogawa, Gucci suddenly ducked his pudgy little self down behind somebody's garden wall and peeked out, as though studying the river. The stream stretched off in either direction. It was lined with bushes that seemed to be concealing boys who were crouching here and there. I could barely see them, just silhouettes, but I could tell that something dark was moving down there in the shadows. I guess I assumed it was boys, since we were in the middle of Armageddon, but it might have been some other low, repulsive life-form. Then I saw beams of light flickering in the gloom. Flashlights. So it was boys—not monsters—out to make the most of the chaos. But then again, I guess "monsters" wasn't far off. They were fighting down there in the bushes, but they were doing it in dead silence. No shouting or screaming, no sound at all, even though I was just above them. But the silence didn't make it any less scary. I could tell someone was being beaten to a pulp down there in the dark. Which was probably what would happen to us, Gucci and me, if they caught us here. I mean, why not? To begin with, I was a girl—fair game in any Armageddon—and one who'd been singled out on the Voice of Heaven for special treatment, and to top it all off, my father had somehow become goofy TV personality Yuzo Gucci. At this point I noticed that Gucci himself was waving to me, and then he finally came out from behind the wall and into the street that ran along the raised bank of the river.

The boys were just below us in the bushes. Flashlight beams scudded along the bank, grazing Gucci as he made his way along the road. It seemed pretty risky to me, but Gucci was on the move, so I had no choice but to follow. Crouching down, we hurried along as fast as we could, and the "Gods" and "Angels" seemed to take no notice of us. They were probably too occupied with the damage they were doing down in the bushes. But the flashlights continued to sweep back and forth across our path, darting along the road and jutting up at the sky. At last we turned off, leaving the river and angling down in the direction of the main road. There wasn't a car to be seen on the street. Everybody must be holed up at home, afraid to go out. Duh. Yet here I was wandering around with Yuzo Gucci, looking for his car. What the FUCK was I thinking? We finally came to the main road, and there we could see a single car, parked at the curb, lights on, engine running. And somebody sitting in the driver's seat, looking this way. More surprises: even from this distance I could see it was none other than famous has-been guitarist Fuyuki Moto. He must have escaped from the same nightmare talk show that had sent me Gucci. Fucking Fuyuki Moto was sitting behind the wheel of Gucci's car, waiting for us with a worried look on his face. The same car I'd heard scattering people like bowling pins? Maybe Moto had been the driver? Maybe it was his car? Anyway, as soon as he came into view, Gucci straightened up and made a dash for the car. I followed. He hopped in the passenger's seat and I tried to get in back, but I suddenly realized it was pretty crowded back there—packed, in fact, with the entire cast of *Your Hit Parade*. What the FUCK? The show had been canceled long ago, so what was the whole crowd doing hanging out in the back of this car? Well, for one thing they were making it really hard for me to get in. I told the nearest has-been to move over, but when I looked, the has-been turned out to be the now-and-future Governor of Tokyo, Shintaro Ishihara, everybody's favorite crazy right-wing pol. It occurred to me to wonder what the hell the fucking *governor* was doing in *here* with the city going to hell out *there*. But one thing was for sure, he wasn't moving over much. "Sorry, full up," he snapped. "Try some other car." To tell the truth, it hurt a little to be dissed like that by the governor, maybe even more because he was dressed up like a factory worker or something. And there wasn't much point in telling him there *wasn't* another car. Even after Gucci asked him real nicely to make room for me, he wouldn't budge. "If she can't get in, she can't get in," he chanted. "What will '*can't*' mean if she *does* in the end?" someone else asked. And then celebrity warfare broke out. "Then why don't *you* get out?" shouted Emily Henmi, yet another *Your Hit Parade* regular, pushing the governor from behind. Ishihara shouted and squirmed, but in the end Emily managed to pry him loose from the seat and shove him out the door. "Hop in, Aiko," she said, beckoning to me, and I did just that. "What's the world *coming* to?" Ishihara shouted, and then he wandered over to the railing of a nearby bridge. Staring down into the dark, he shouted again at the boys in the bushes. "And you *assholes*, what the FUCK are you doing down there?" He was getting more and more worked up, as only the governor can, and before we knew it he had run around the guard rail and disappeared down the bank into the dark. Oh boy. Take care, Mr. Governor. I was a little worried, but then who was going to mess with Shintaro Ishihara in full rut?

I settled down next to Emily. "Thanks," I said. "Don't mention it," she said, laughing. I'd always thought of her as just another famous nobody, but her stock had suddenly shot up in my book. Now that I was seeing her up close, I realized she was totally cute. Beautiful skin, beautiful hair, perfect makeup. Wonder how she did that? "We're off!" shouted Fuyuki Moto, and the car lurched forward. "Where are we going?" I wondered aloud. "First stop, Chofu Station," said Gucci. Chofu Station? Right smack into the middle of Armageddon? "Don't worry," Gucci reassured me. "They've moved on, and the middle school kids have all died or run away." You're kidding? "No, really." Then Fuyuki Moto spoke up. "The road's a little bumpy up ahead. Hang on, everybody!" What? *DOKKON! DOKKON!* A terrible jolt went through the car and its load of celebrities, as though we had run over something. We inched forward and then *DOKKON! DOKKON!* all over again. What was that? "Middler, I'm afraid. But don't *worry*! They're sturdy little fuckers." Not *that* sturdy, I thought, not enough to survive that! "See," said Fuyuki Moto, pointing out the back window. "Looks okay to me." I turned around in time to see a kid about my age struggling to get back to his feet.

When he was standing again, I could see it was a boy wearing a school uniform. He bent down to brush off his pants—and he was apparently unhurt. Fuyuki was right, middlers are tough. Super tough. *DOKKON! DOKKON!...DOKKON! DOKKON! DOKKON!* We raced off toward the station, plowing over kid after kid like so many bumps in the road. I leaned forward, poking my head between Gucci and Moto, and peered out through the windshield. The highway ran straight to the station, with bumps lined up as far as the eye could see. Most looked like middle school road kill from Armageddon, though there might have been a few adults mixed in. I kept an eye out for my brother, but it was kind of hard to make out faces. Then I saw a bus coming from the other direction, running over the bodies in the street just like we were. Were middle school kids bus-resistant? I somehow doubted it, but who knows. As the bus passed us, I scanned the faces of the passengers, hoping to find my brother. But no such luck. A moment later, we pulled into the roundabout in front of the station. It was completely quiet, no middle school kids or anyone else scattered on the ground. Nothing at all to mark the passing of Armageddon. Just Chofu Station, same as it always was—except with nobody going in or out or any sign of station staff. They must all still be hiding. I climbed out of the car, but nobody else followed me. Gucci rolled down the window on the passenger side. "You should head on down to City Hall in Shinjuku," he said. "Everybody's going to be there." City Hall? Had somebody suddenly called a town meeting? And what, I asked, looking back at Gucci, was he going to do? "Daddy's going to look for Governor Ishihara," he said. The governor? Sorry about losing him. "Not your fault, Aiko," Gucci said. "But are you going to be okay on your own?" Not really, I thought, but I didn't see what good it would do to tell him that. "Should I just show up at City Hall and tell them I'm from Chofu?" "Sounds like a plan," Gucci answered. "The folks in charge will tell you where to go." Okay, got it, thanks. "Take care of yourself," I said, and Gucci gave me one last well-tanned smile. "Don't fret, sweetie. Looks like Armageddon won't last much longer. See you, then," he said. See you. And with that, the big black car stuffed with Gucci and Moto and Emily Henmi and the entire cast of *Your Hit Parade* made a quick circuit around the rotary and disappeared down the road.

What time was it? I checked my phone: still just five-thirty. Wonder what time the meeting would start? Anyway, might as well go buy a ticket. I went down into the undercroft that led to the ticket machines. A man was coming toward me in the narrow passage, but there was no one else around. Tense. With just the two of us in the whole place, I could hardly pass by without looking at him. It made me terribly nervous. Shit, shit, shit, shit, shit, shit! Keep your head down, just walk by, don't look up. But as we were passing, he said, "Excuse me." "Yes?" I said, looking up. What a truly gross guy! Shaggy hair, pale, geeky face, pink shirt tucked into geeky pants—and somehow strangely, geekily familiar? Where had I seen him before? No idea. Maybe I was just imagining it. Then I realized he looked just like Bondo Oki, another TV star, or what passes for one on the late-night network offerings.

"Is this the way to City Hall?" he asked.

"You're headed in the right direction," I said, "but you have to get back on the train. You're only in Chofu." Shit! We were going the same way. Oh well. It was a little lonely around here. The pink-shirted fellow just thanked me and turned to go, as though he hadn't heard a word I'd said. Whatever. Who wanted to hang out with a geek, especially a gender-ambiguous one? The guy was pudgy, maybe even busty, with a little gold ring on "his" left hand.

Maybe the guy was a girl? Or gay? Whatever. Gross.

As soon as I got up to the platform, a train pulled into the station, and there were actually some people on it. What a relief. Armageddon refugees? The train was one of those long-distance jobs, not the normal commuter version, with pairs of seats facing each other. I made my way down the aisle, checking out the other passengers—mostly parents with really noisy kids. The train started up before I could find a seat, and as I staggered through the car I wondered whether I should have stayed home to wait for my brother. Then for some reason it occurred to me that this might be some sort of special refugee train and that my brother might even be on it. But as I looked around almost expecting to see him, a woman's voice came on the loudspeaker. "This is the 5:30 p.m. Hikari Express No. 336, bound for Tottori Prefecture," she said. Shit! Somehow I'd got on the wrong train. This was a bullet train, heading west—the exact opposite direction from the commuter line that should have been taking me into town. Why hadn't I realized right away? No Keio Line train has seats that face each other. But now what was I going to do? I'd have to get off at the next stop—though they might make me pay anyway. Did I have enough money if they did? I stopped in the aisle and took out my wallet—two thousand yen. Was that enough? Of course it wasn't! This was no joke. I decided I needed to find the conductor and explain what had happened. Could I promise I'd send him the money later? Outside the window, the city was disappearing and we were racing through fields and rice paddies at bullet train speed. Shit, shit, SHIT! Had we already left Tokyo? Where were we? I reached the end of the aisle, slid open the door, and stood for a moment looking out the window in the compartment between cars. The cluster of skyscrapers in West Shinjuku was barely visible in the distance, across a wide expanse of fields. What the fuck? Whatever. I should at least try to reach my brother. He was probably home by now, waiting for me. I took out my phone and called him. He picked up right away. "Where are you?" he asked as soon as he heard my voice. "Sorry!" I yelled into the phone. "It's AWFUL!" "What's awful?" "I got on the wrong train!" "What do you mean? What train?" "I don't know. I think we're headed for Tottori!" "Tottori? Why are you going to Tottori? Do you have the money for the ticket?" "I don't know! No! I've only got two thousand yen!" "Then how are you going to get back?" "I'm not GOING all the way to Tottori!" "Okay, but make sure they don't catch you at the station. It could get pretty scary." "What do you mean?" "A friend of mine got way out somewhere without a ticket and when they caught him they made him pay big time." "You're kidding. How much?" "You know how much they collect from the family when some suicide case throws himself in front of the train? Well, more than that!" "No shit?" "No shit! Two, three hundred million, at least." I was starting to feel faint. But hold on a minute. My dad was Yuzo Gucci, right? A guy as famous as Gucci must have that kind of money stashed away somewhere. Or maybe not? Maybe not. Maybe we'd have to sell our house to cover the ticket. Whoa! "Whoa!" I said out loud. "You said it. So whatever you do, don't let them catch you at the station!" "Okay, but what about the conductor on the train?" "That's even worse. You'd better lock yourself in the toilet and wait until you get to the next stop." "Okay, I'll try that," I told him. Three hundred million was no laughing matter. I didn't see how my brother or even Gucci himself could help me out of a jam like this. As I headed for the bathroom, I glanced back into the car. The conductor was stopped in the aisle talking to a girl—really more like an anime character than any girl I'd ever seen—and then she stood up and pointed in my direction. Shit, shit, SHIT! Shitty anime girl! Remind me to deal with her later. "Yes, Mr. Conductor, sir, I remember seeing somebody like that. She went that way...!" Fuck! And now Mr. Conductor, sir, was heading in my direction. Too late to hide in the bathroom here. I'd have to run through the next car and find another one. When I looked back to see if he was coming, I realized the conductor wasn't really a conductor—now he looked more like a Mafia don, and he seemed to have a bunch of his boys following him through the car. Whoa! Maybe this was no ordinary Bullet train after all—it was starting to seem more like a trap, laid especially to catch...me! I ran through the door into the next car. Halfway down the aisle, I glanced over my shoulder just in time to see the don and his muscle coming through the door. They were wearing flashy suits—Italian probably—and they were giving me the evil eye. When the don's jacket fell open, I caught a glimpse of a gun strapped to his chest. Shit! If they catch me, I'm toast! At this point I realized I no longer cared what the people around me thought—and I was just noticing they were all foreigners, anyway. So I started screaming in English. "Help! Somebody help me! They're trying to kill me! Call the police!" I thought my English was pretty good, but they just sat there staring at me like I was some geeky inscrutable Japanese person. Pretty cold. "Help! Please help me!" Still nothing, despite my best pronunciation. Were they just going to sit there and watch me get shot? I bolted down the aisle, through the door and the compartment between the cars, and into the next one beyond. But as I started down this new aisle, I realized there was another group of Mafioso coming at me from the other direction. I stopped and held up my hands. The first don and his thugs were coming up behind me. Totally screwed! I could feel my legs shaking and my knees beginning to buckle. But maybe there were too many witnesses? They couldn't just shoot me right here in the aisle...could they? I still had a chance. "Somebody help me! Please!" I yelled again. But this time was different. I heard a noise and looked around to see a guy in a nice suit. "Get down!" he yelled, and I instantly hit the deck. There were three loud bangs and a spurt of blood, and then right above me I saw James Gandolfini with three bullet holes in his chest. He fell like a ton of bricks, and that great big gut of his came to rest on my right arm. Warm and heavy. I pulled free and pried his pistol out of his hand. Just then, the door slid open again and Tom Sizemore was standing there—and somehow it was suddenly obvious that Sizemore had been the Mafia don all along. I aimed my gun—Tony Soprano's gun—and Sizemore aimed his back at me, an ugly grin spreading across his ugly mug. He obviously thought I wouldn't be able to bring myself to fire. He was wrong there. I put my finger on the trigger and pulled, but the action was sticky and I couldn't squeeze off a shot.

But as I was fumbling with the gun, a loud voice yelled "FBI! Don't move!" and in the next instant the windows of the car seemed to vaporize, and several dozen men in black paramilitary gear burst into the car. They surrounded the Mafia guys and covered them with machine guns. There was dead silence for a moment as I lay there aiming up at Tom Sizemore. But Tom wasn't looking at me anymore. He was glancing around, sizing up the new situation—a whole world of trouble. Yet he still had that grin on his face. "Freeze!" the FBI loudspeaker ordered. "Drop your guns!" But Tom wasn't listening. He smiled even bigger and spun around on the SWAT team; but before he could get off a shot, he was blown back down the car by a spray of bullets. "Fuck!" one of his guys yelled, and the rest of them reached for their guns. "Freeze!" the bullhorn blared again, but in the next instant a hail of machine gun fire ripped into the Mafioso and they fell where they stood, riddled with bullet holes.

Like they say, don't mess with the FBI.

The man in the suit helped me up—and I realized he was the guy who runs the control room in *Mission Impossible*, though I can never remember his name. Anyway, I got off the train with the SWAT team, and it turned out we were at the edge of a desert, a totally barren sea of sand and scrub brush leading off to a sheer cliff in the distance. A network of deep ravines flanked the tracks on both sides, with these deep blue rivers flowing at the bottom. Weird-looking place. And how was I supposed to get home now? The SWAT team was climbing into their helicopter and getting ready to head off, and the Mission Impossible guy had disappeared somewhere. Shit. The rest of the passengers were filing from the train and wandering off in every direction—and not even one of them was Japanese. I was beginning to feel totally desperate. I tried to get help, but no one seemed to understand me. A dark-skinned woman with lots of luggage was standing nearby, so I asked in my best English where I could find the station, but she just started babbling in a language I couldn't even identify. Shit! Where was I? What was this? It almost looked like America. Had I somehow wound up in Mexico or someplace? If so, then I was really pretty screwed. More and more screwed every minute. The FBI? But why hadn't they escorted me home? Pretty half-assed rescue, if you ask me. And now what? I didn't even have any money. Or know anybody around here, wherever "here" was. Like I said, totally screwed. So finally, having nothing better to do, I fell in behind some other passengers as they wandered away from the train. After plodding along for a while, I came up to a stark-naked boy and girl standing in the middle of the dusty dirt path. Well maybe kids in this part of the world go around butt-naked all the time. But somehow I knew I shouldn't stop too long, that if I did, somebody might come along and strip me too. Without any luggage, I was making better time than the other passengers in the line, so I scrambled off through the cactus or baobab or whatever the hell it was. Then in the distance I saw a man in a suit with white hair. Steve Martin? Gray suit, jacket tucked under his arm. And next to Steve, a fat man in a puffy blue down jacket. Hell no! John Candy too? What luck! This was just like the moment in *Planes, Trains & Automobiles* when they were headed back to Steve Martin's house, so if I just followed them, I would at least end up somewhere in the States, which would be better than this hellhole. I started running, but for some reason I couldn't catch up with them, even though they were walking and I was running. Really fast. I started sweating like a pig, and since I never really get any exercise, I pooped out pretty quick. I was telling my legs to run, but they just didn't seem to be listening, and by now Steve Martin and John Candy were off in the distance on top of a cliff on the other side of a river with no way across. Pretty much just like the climax of *Indiana Jones and the Temple of Doom*—except no rope bridge. You're kidding me! But as I stood on my side of the gorge wondering how Steve and John got across, they were already disappearing into the shadow of the cliff. Damn it! Left behind again. "Hey!" I called after them, but it was too late, and there I was, alone. Alone? I looked around and it was true. Nobody but me. I'd been so busy following Steve and John that I hadn't noticed that all the other passengers had gone off somewhere else. The train, too, was now only a tiny line on the horizon; and what good would it do anyway, going back to a train that was no longer running? On the other hand, if I stayed by the tracks, at least I could catch the next train that came along. That was probably the best plan: wait for a train and get dropped off somewhere. Better that than end up sleeping out here by the gorge. But just as I decided I would go back, I heard someone call my name. "Aiko!

Hey! Aiko!" A voice that could speak *Japanese* calling my name! A voice that sounded familiar. I ran back to the gorge, and there, a hundred yards away, on top of the cliff silhouetted against the blue sky, stood a boy, waving in my direction. Akihiko Sano.

Sano?

What was Sano doing here? Everybody's been looking for him. What was he doing out here in the middle of nowhere America or Mexico or wherever the hell we were?

"Hey!" I called, waving to him.

"Hey!" he called again and waved back. "Come on up!"

"How?" I yelled. "There's no bridge!"

"There's an airplane right over there!" he called. "Use that!"

I walked toward the spot where he was pointing and saw he was right—sort of. Hidden behind a nearby pile of rock was a helicopter, not a plane. One large propeller on top—and totally rusted out. It must have crash-landed here ages ago.

"You mean this?" I called up to Sano.

"Yes, yes," he shouted. I studied the heap of twisted metal. A one-man helicopter, but with the cockpit mostly ripped away and the seat in tatters. It was half buried in sand, and the iron arm and shaft were red with rust. No way this bucket of shit was going to fly. "Hop in and get up here!" Sano called.

In this? Seriously?

What the hell? I slid into the ruined seat, which was a bit tricky since the chopper was tipped over in the sand, but as I pushed into the backrest, the whole thing seemed to pop upright out of the dune. Okay. But was there any fuel in the tank? I looked down at the instrument panel next to the control stick—and realized that there were pedals below, pretty much like on a bicycle. Was that really how you flew this thing? Pedals? Seriously? I brushed away as much sand as I could and grabbed the stick. Then I tried pushing on one of the pedals. Pretty sticky. I pushed harder. Still not much give. But slowly they began to move under my feet; and as they did, the propeller just above my head began to spin. I got situated and pumped a little faster. The propeller spun faster too. I started pedaling for real and the propeller began to whirr. Was this thing actually going to fly? I pumped as hard as I could, and there was a whooshing sound, and a gust of hot air shot down on me. Unbelievable. By now the propeller was spinning so fast it was scary. *Bwuuuuuuuun!* The copter bucked sideways for a second and rose up in the air. I barely moved the stick, but it lurched forward and I was about to crash into a tree. So I yanked the stick toward me and shot up even higher, barely missing the treetop. I eased off on the stick and leveled out. Okay, Aiko, you can *do* this! I rotated the stick slightly and headed the chopper over the gorge, then slowed a bit as I got closer to the cliff. Using Sano as a point to steer by, I headed up and over the top.

"Awesome!" he yelled, waving up at me. I didn't really have a free hand to wave back. "But whatever you do," I heard him call, "don't look down." Shit. I was already looking down—and realizing that the blue river at the bottom of the gorge wasn't really a river at all, it was more sky, sky in the opposite direction from the first sky. And somehow I could tell that I was seeing the souls of lots of people coming and going in this river of sky. Sky below, and crowds of souls milling around. They were definitely human shaped, bluish white—almost translucent—and there were lots of them trailing along, like they were swimming…and they were pretty much nude.

Was this for real? I was seeing dead people. Lots of them.

And they were all going off to the right, down the valley. I spun the helicopter around in that direction, and in the distance I could see this spooky red sunset and below it an ominous, purple night sky. The souls were heading off in that direction, toward the white boundary between the bright sunlight and the dark sky below…or maybe the boundary was actually formed by the river of pale blue souls itself as it trailed off into the distance.

"Hey! Over here!" Sano was calling again, and I swung the helicopter around in his direction. I was pretty close now, but his face looked fuzzy somehow.

Was it really Sano? If it was, he should be missing a toe…

I tried to check his foot, but it was blurry too. Not that I could have seen his toes at this distance—through his shoes…

"Over here!" he was still yelling. "That's right."

It must be Sano. But what was he doing here? Why didn't he go home to Chofu?

I suddenly had a bad feeling about all this. Something didn't seem quite right…So I pulled back on the stick a bit, not wanting to get to him too quickly, and hovered between the two cliffs. Then I looked around over my shoulder, thinking maybe I should go back the way I'd come, and I got another shock. Carved on the face of the cliff on the other side, in letters as big as a house, was a message.

Stop!
Come back!

Right there on the cliff—in perfectly good Japanese no less. Who could have written it? And there was more, carved in the enormous rock face.

Come back! Don't go over there! Don't even *look* over there!

Over there? Over here? Which was which? What the fuck?

That Sano over there is a fake. The real one is over here.

Real? Fake? Over where?

I turned back to look at Sano. Was he "over there" or "over here"? And was he the real Sano?

Was the real one back "over there," which he was calling "over here"? I was getting a little confused.

But I couldn't see anyone on that side.

I glanced back at the cliff, but now the message had changed.

Not over there, Aiko! Listen to me! Come back! Hurry!

Who did he think he was, ordering me around like that?

But he did know my name.

Who could carve those huge letters in a cliff like that—and then erase them and write something else?

It was then that I realized that the Sano "over there" was still waving and calling for me to "come back," but now he was laughing like an idiot. That *must* be Sano. But was he doing the writing too?

I didn't know what to think, but I knew it was totally incredible. But also impossible.

So what to do? I flew over toward the cliff over "here," and even though there was no one to talk to, since Sano—real or fake—was over "there," I shouted at the cliff.

"Who are you?"

There was a pause and then the words carved on the face of the cliff vanished and new ones appeared. No one filled in the old ones and no one carved the new ones. The cliff seemed to be carving itself. Never underestimate the good old US of A—if that's where I was.

It's me, Yoji!

No way! This was too much. My head was starting to hurt.

Stop messing around and get back over here! Don't go over there!

Hear me? Get back here!

"How are you doing this exactly?" I called.

What? I have somebody who does it for me. Stop asking stupid questions and get back over here!

"Coming!"

It was Yoji talking after all. Was I really not going to go? I banked and headed back in his direction. You do the math: Yoji vs. Sano? Bye-bye, Sano!

But then as I looked back for one last glance at Sano—I got *another* shock. His face, which until now had been hard to make out—sort of a blank, actually—was suddenly crystal clear, and I could see his eyes blazing, his mouth torn open, and some weird gas puffing out of his nose.

"Wait! Don't be stupid, Aiko!"

It sounded just like something Sano would say. But Sano wasn't Sano anymore. He'd turned into a totally creepy monster. Scary! Way scary! Time to get out of here. But as I started to pedal like mad, Sano Monster reached out toward me with both hands—and unlike normal reaching out, unlike normal *hands*, his seemed to keep coming and coming at me. His arms were actually stretching. Gya! He was some kind of ghost. I could see that now. It was Sano and yet not Sano. Not human Sano anyway. I wasn't sure what it was, but it was trying to drag me back "there" and I totally didn't want to go! I could see now that he was the bad guy! Why had it been so hard to figure out before? "Over here" we have Yoji—so by definition "over there" had to be the bad guy. But all this was going through my mind really, really quick—because the rest of me was totally busy pedaling. I glanced back and could see Sano's white arms stretching out—and out and out and out and out and out toward my little chopper. Scary Sano! Scary scary scary scary scary! Stop it! Leave me alone! I could tell I was about to start crying. But this was no time to cry. If those hands got me, I would never get back to "this" side, to Yoji's side, and then I'd never see him again. And I couldn't let that happen!

Sano could just fuck off and die!

But of course! That was it! I suddenly understood.

Sano had done just that—died. The Sano waving to me on the cliff was already an ex-Sano, and "over there" was the side of the dead. "Over here," Yoji's side, was where living people—well—lived. Shit! So then that river with all the souls swimming along down there—must be the Styx.

Good grief! I'd been about to cross the River Styx! Sano, that shit, had been trying to lure me across—which would *not* have been a good idea!

I glanced back. Sano was still standing on top of the cliff, reaching those spooky arms toward me. And they were getting closer and closer. I wasn't out of the woods yet!

"Help me, Yoji!" I screamed.

Sorry, I'm afraid I can't.

Well, at least he didn't beat around the bush.

But don't give up!

Uh…okay. I won't.

Don't give up, Aiko!

I didn't. I pedaled like crazy. Pedal pedal pedal pedal pedal pedal pedal!

But Sano's hands were gaining on me. They were just a few inches away. So I pedaled even harder, like totally crazy hard, like it was the end if I didn't—duh!

Come on, Aiko!

Shit! It's no good. I'm not going to make it, Yoji!

Hold on! You can do it!

Forget it! I'm telling you I can't. Don't keep saying I can!

And at that point Sano's creepy weird hands were just about to grab hold of the tail of my helicopter.

"Keep your fucking hands *off*, Sano!"

Jump!

What?

Don't worry, just jump!

I looked down—nothing but the sky at the bottom of the gorge and the river of dead souls flowing through it. A hundred yards below. Or more.

I could barely see from the sweat pouring off my face.

"I can't, Yoji!"

It's okay! Just jump!

Okay? No way! It isn't okay *at all*! You think *you* could take a swan dive into a river of dead souls, Yoji?

Don't worry! I'll catch you!

Well why didn't you say so? That's a whole different story. But where are you? Are you dead? If you are, then I don't really mind dying.

I'm not dead, you idiot! Stop talking nonsense and *jump!*

Noooooo! Shit! He got me. Sano had grabbed hold of my helicopter, and he was beginning to drag me back "there." When I turned to look, those totally weirdo blazing eyes were getting closer and closer. Shit!

You idiot, Aiko! If you're going

to jump, do it now!

"I'm holding you responsible, Yoji!" I screamed.

Then I pushed up out of the seat and jumped—straight toward the river of dead souls at the bottom of the sky spread out below...

Byuuuuuuuuuuuuuuuuuuu!

I fell faster and faster, the cliff racing by next to me. The blue river of the dead came rushing up toward me, and as I got closer I could see that it consisted of an unbelievable number of souls— too many, in fact, even for all the people who had ever lived in the whole world. But then it occurred to me that maybe it wasn't just people, maybe these were the souls of animals and plants too. Or maybe even the souls of aliens?

But was this really the time to be worrying about stuff like that? I was falling and was going to die too!

Falling into the sky to die!

Diving into the river of the dead!

What could be lamer than that?

But just as the river filled up my whole field of vision, just as I was about to plunge in, I felt someone grab my collar, and my fall began to slow. Finally I stopped, right in midair.

Saaaaafe!

I craned my neck around, calling Yoji's name, but when I looked, it wasn't Yoji holding me but that weird guy—or girl?—I had met in the underground passage at Chofu Station, the geeky one with the long hair and the pink shirt that looked just like Bondo Oki.

What the fuck was he—she?—doing here?

"Who the fuck are *you*?" I said.

"Calm down, calm down," said a husky but shrill voice—still no way to tell whether it was male or female—and then I felt myself being lifted up by the collar.

Or maybe I was floating up, along with my geeky rescuer.

Up and up.

Suspended by the scruff of my neck, like a kitten in its mother's mouth, I floated up through the clouds, back to the valley where I'd been before, though both Sano and the helicopter had vanished.

Good riddance.

I was relieved, starting to feel a little more like myself.

"Who are you?" I asked, trying to sound a little nicer this time.

"Me? My name is Tansetsu Sakurazuki."

Tansetsu Sakurazuki? What kind of name was that? Sounded like the pen name of some bogus manga writer. And he looked the part too.

But even knowing the name, I still wasn't sure about the gender.

"And what exactly do you do?" I asked.

"I'm a fortune-teller."

That figured.

"And where do you tell these fortunes?"

"At Odaiba—in Tokyo—but that hardly matters now, I would think."

"It matters to me. You look pretty suspicious."

Sakurazuki let out a sigh.

"Well, Miss Aiko Katsura, your suspicion is the reason my rescue didn't go as smoothly as I would have liked."

"Rescue?"

"Just come back with me and all will be explained."

"So was it you who saved me from the Mafia guys on the train?"

"Guilty as charged. I've been looking out for you in a number of guises."

"Were you Emily Henmi too?"

"No, during the Emily and Gucci kidnap caper, I was Shintaro Ishihara, governor of Tokyo. You really shouldn't have gotten in that car."

He was Shintaro Ishihara? What was going on?

"That whole episode was a little dicey. If it weren't for the help I received from your little friend Yoji Kaneda, we might have lost you."

"Yoji! Where'd he get to anyway? Why are you here and not him?"

I can't go over there, Aiko! So make nice and say thank you to Mr. Sakurazuki.

"So *that's* how Mr. Kaneda has been communicating with you, in those big letters on the cliff. It's the best he can do—though I suppose you don't really mind, do you Aiko, since it's Mr. Kaneda? I suspect you'll forgive his rather vulgar 'shouting.'"

What was he talking about? Had he somehow figured out how I felt about Yoji?

But he had! Shit! And now Yoji would know too!

"Yoji!" I shouted.

What?

"Do you like me?"

What?!

"Hold on, Miss Katsura, are you sure—"

"It's okay, I need to know."

"But please wait just a minute, until we get to the top of the cliff over there."

"But when we get there, I won't be able to see what Yoji's writing."

"I'm sure you'll manage somehow…"

"No, I want to see what he writes," I told him.

I was totally embarrassed, ready to crawl in a hole. But I'd had these feelings—this love—for six years now, and I needed to know whether Yoji felt anything in return.

"Yoji? Do you like me? Do you have any feelings for me at all?"

He *had* saved my life, after all.

At least he hadn't wanted me to die!

"Yoji? Answer me!"

What? Why are you asking? Can't we just be friends?

So, that was that.

Whatever. I knew he was telling the truth. Nobody lies about a thing like that. Not that I wouldn't have minded if he had—if he'd told me he liked me even if it was a lie—but he was Yoji and Yoji had to tell the truth. Shit, shit, shit!

But at least now I knew.

"Thanks, Yoji. See you around."

I reached back and yanked the collar of my shirt loose from Sakurazuki's sweaty hand and sent myself falling again, back deep into the sky.

Byuuuuuuuuuuuuuuuuuuuuuuuuun!

Sakurazuki came flying after me as I fell, but he looked totally GROSS—so I kicked his ugly face in midair to stop him from saving me. After I landed the kick, he fell way behind and I lost sight of him. Fine with me.

Totally fine with me if I died just about now. Now that I knew for sure, what did I have to live for?

The Way of Love was closed to me, so what was the point of living? Enough already. I knew that only an idiot would give up this easily, but anything was better than living with all this shame and pain. Dying was actually easier. Sorry! Sorry I didn't have more will to live! But what the fuck? Don't be mad at me for copping out like this. It was just that it all happened a little too quick: my declaration of love, Yoji's rejection, and now my swift demise. But that was all right with me.

I loved you, Yoji.

Ever since—you know when. I only had eyes for Yoji. You were all I wanted in the whole wide world. What a shame it wasn't meant to be.

Bye-bye.

Ahhh. But what was going to happen to me now, falling up into the sky?

The Forest

Morning comes early in Hadetbra.

My father and mother leave for work before dawn. My older brother, Olle, hops up just as they are going—he has soccer every morning at school. He eats his breakfast and then heads off to practice, kicking the ball all the way. So I am quite alone by six o'clock when I finally rouse myself. In point of fact, the mothers and fathers in the other two houses in Hadetbra also leave for work before dawn, so the children who are left behind get out of bed and gather for breakfast. We all agree that the meal tastes better when we eat together. We refer to our little group as an "eating club," and we like to think it is a very grown-up sort of gathering, just the sort of thing our parents would do if they didn't have to hurry off to work. We call it the Hadetbra Morning Eating Club.

The members of our little club include Hejdanatt and Adju, the sisters who live next door on one side, and Nulla and Inte, the brothers on the other, their little sister Nej, and me—I'm Kerstin.

Nulla and Inte love soccer too, and I'm sure they would like to be on the team with Olle, but they are both terrible sleepyheads and seem to prefer to stay in bed hugging their pillows rather than get up early to kick the ball with the boys at school.

Today again, our mothers left breakfast for us, and we brought what they had made and gathered to eat it at one table. But today was just slightly different. Usually, we eat at Nulla and Inte's house, since they have the biggest family and the biggest table. But today the sky was so very blue, and the clouds were racing across it in such wonderful shapes, that it was hard to stay indoors. Someone suggested we have a picnic, so we carried the table out to the garden and had our breakfast in the open air.

And what a lovely breakfast it was! So lovely I found myself wondering why we didn't do this every day. The sausages and milk and eggs were even more delicious than usual—perhaps they were delighted to be set outdoors too. The goat cheese dissolved softly on my tongue, the wonderful flavor rippling through my mouth. Cheese this fresh and soft is better eaten just as it is, rather than spread on bread. Everyone seemed to be enjoying it. Nulla had piled a ridiculous mound on a slice of toast, more than he could possibly fit in his mouth, and when he tried, he planted the end of his nose in the pile. As I watched, quite appalled, his little brother Inte reached out for the cheese to repeat the trick. So I slapped his hand. I shudder to think how our meals would deteriorate if I weren't here to counter the bad influence of Nulla and Inte. But I suppose all boys have their naughty side. Which is why we girls have to keep an eye on them. When I told them they mustn't play with their food, Hejdanatt chimed in to say that it was a waste of perfectly good cheese. And Adju and Nej had to add their own two cents after her.

Today was a wonderful, wonderful day—the first day of summer vacation. As soon as we had finished our breakfast, Nulla and Inte began looking around for something to do. It was, they said, much too much trouble to go all the way to school to play soccer. How about swimming in the river? Or having an adventure in the forest? Perhaps we should go tease Lorna's dog. Or go hunting for insects. The boys tossed out ideas one after another.

Now that we had finished our meal, we girls needed to decide what we wanted to do as well. Adju and Hejdanatt and Nej all looked at me. Since the weather was so fine, I was in favor of going to the river or the woods to play with the boys. Still, I knew that Adju didn't like to join in their games since she thought they could get too rough. Her older sister, Hejdanatt, on the other hand, was as rough and competitive as they come.

I told the boys that they mustn't go into the Western Forest.

Of course they wanted to know why.

Because, I explained, a terrifying monster had recently made its home there.

As I might have foreseen, this news only excited their curiosity. "What kind of monster?" Nulla wanted to know.

"The kind that snatches children and cuts them up into little pieces," I told them.

Inte was properly frightened now, but Nulla's eyes sparkled. "And then eats them?" he wanted to know.

"Apparently not," I told him. "The monster takes them deep into the forest, all in pieces, and leaves them alone to die ever so slowly."

At this last bit of information I finally detected a look of fear in Nulla's eyes.

A moment later, however, the boys were busy with their silly games. They pinched each other's arms and cheeks, apparently conducting experiments to see how much it might hurt to be cut up by the monster.

First Nulla took the skin near Inte's elbow between his thumb and forefinger and gave it a hard squeeze.

Ouch, ouch!

Inte conceded immediately, apparently in real pain.

Then it was Nulla's turn.

Inte chose a particularly soft spot on his upper arm and squeezed as hard as he could. Nulla clenched his teeth. "Give up?" Inte asked. Nulla shook his head. He's a very competitive boy, and he wasn't likely to surrender that easily.

So Inte found a spot on the white skin of his thigh, protruding from his little shorts, and pinched there with his other hand. The expression on Nulla's face was almost relaxed now. "Is that the best you can do?" he asked. To look at them, you might have thought Inte was the one being pinched. He closed his eyes and squeezed with all his might. Nulla tensed and his mouth came open in a great circle, as though a cry were about to emerge, but he remained silent. He merely stood there, eyes closed and mouth open, and forced himself to bear up under the pain. It was an impressive feat to behold.

Next Nulla found a fork that was lying on the table and handed it to Inte. "Try using this," he told his brother, laughing merrily. But Inte looked shocked, and we girls, watching nearby, were horrified.

"Stop, Nulla," I told him. But he just laughed again and said that such a little fork would never pierce the skin, that it would do nothing more than make a slight impression.

"Have a go," he told Inte.

Inte held the fork in his hand, but he looked completely lost.

"Stop," I said again. "You'll get hurt."

"Don't worry," Nulla said. "I'm sure he'll be gentle."

"But why do you want him to?" I asked.

"Because I want to know how the children feel when the

monster cuts them," he said.

This was hardly an explanation. Why would anyone intentionally ask you to hurt him? But as I stood puzzling over his answer, he urged his brother again.

"Just a little stab, Inte," he said. Inte closed his eyes and, gripping the fork in his hands, he planted it in Nulla's abdomen. "Doesn't hurt a bit," said Nulla. "Look," he added, rolling up his shirt to expose the soft white skin of his belly. "Do it again," he said.

Inte was clearly upset, but what could he do, with Nulla egging him on like that? He closed his eyes, clutched the fork tighter, and slowly pushed it into Nulla's stomach.

"Harder," said Nulla.

Inte pushed the fork and at last the tip buried itself in Nulla's skin.

"Still nothing," Nulla said, so Inte planted it deeper. By now the tines of the fork had vanished into Nulla—though he showed no signs of distress.

"Harder, harder," he ordered.

I wondered how he could be standing the pain, but judging from the smile on his face he was much less uncomfortable than when his brother had pinched him a moment ago.

The top of the fork's handle had disappeared into Nulla's belly.

"Nope, nothing," he said. "A fork doesn't hurt at all." Looking terribly relieved, Inte immediately pulled it out. A line of four red dots appeared on Nulla's skin.

Then, in the blink of an eye, Nulla had taken the fork from Inte's hand and replaced it with a knife that had been left on the table.

"Try this instead," he told his brother. The blood seemed to drain from Inte's face.

"Stop it!" I cried.

Nulla laughed. "Don't worry," he said. "It can't be any worse than the fork. Give it a try, Inte. Just like before."

Then he grabbed Inte's hand and pulled the knife straight toward his gut. The flat, silver tip of the blade entered near the marks left by the fork and disappeared slowly under the skin. Nulla's belly must have been very soft, because the blade slid in quite easily as we stood there and watched. I was hypnotized now, unable to look away. The other girls were staring too. Very slowly, Nulla pulled his brother's hand toward him, drawing the blade into his body.

"I can't feel a thing," he said, letting go of Inte's hand at last. "Try pushing it a little deeper."

Inte did as he was told, and the knife disappeared bit by bit into Nulla's belly.

Then, all at once, Nulla, who had maintained an icy calm up to this point, suddenly let out a terrible scream and collapsed into a chair.

Inte, his face instantly gone white, pulled back on the knife, and as he did, Nulla slipped from the chair and onto the floor. Inte tossed the knife aside and bent over his brother. "Nulla!" he cried, and the rest of us rushed over to them. "Nulla! Nulla! Are you all right?" we called, but he just lay there with his eyes closed, his clenched teeth visible between his lips.

Foolish Nulla!

That's what comes of playing with knives!

Nulla! we called again.

But then from somewhere we could suddenly hear an eerie laugh, and when we looked more closely, it was clear that Nulla's shoulders were shaking in time with the sound.

He'd fooled us completely!

I hit him on the back, and his eyes opened in a bright smile. "Gotcha!" he giggled.

We felt relieved and exhausted and crestfallen somehow all at once, and the whole group collapsed in a circle on the ground. Nulla looked around at us, smiling his inimitable smile, but Inte, perhaps still not understanding that his brother had been playing a trick on us, stood over him with a flabbergasted look on his face.

Nulla stood at last. "Gotcha, gotcha," he said and danced away as if to mock us. It was only then that Inte seemed to realize what had happened—but the realization made him suddenly very mad.

"Nulla!" he screamed, chasing after his brother. Nulla just laughed and ran away, followed by the furious Inte; and since it appeared the chase was on, we girls joined in, crying out wildly as we, too, ran after Nulla. Thus it was that the first day of our summer holidays began with an impromptu game of tag.

When we had finished with tag and then hide-and-seek, we returned the plates and bowls we had brought from our kitchens, tidied up the table, and sat down to discuss how to spend the day. In the end, we decided to go down to the river.

The river was full of fish and freshwater crabs, and Nulla and Inte were always anxious to try to catch them—though we girls much preferred to simply look at these creatures as we paddled about in the clear water.

A large trout came swimming up from the bottom and passed right near where I was floating, its body slowly undulating, as though it were showing off its handsome scales. Golden sunlight filtered down, glinting brightly off the fish's belly. It was so pretty that I decided not to tell the boys. The trout sank again below me, swimming majestically away upstream. It occurred to me that the fish must be some powerful being that inhabited the river, and it made me happy to think that I was the only one who had caught a glimpse of it.

I climbed up on the bank and let the bright sun warm my

chilled body for a few minutes, and then we all headed off on a walk downstream. Branches had fallen from the trees and were floating in the river. The boys fished out two that had been smoothed in the water and used them for a swordfight. The girls wandered slowly along the bank, searching for oddly shaped rocks and pretty pebbles. Adju found one that was snow white. It was so pure it seemed almost translucent, like a piece of smoky glass. "Maybe it's a gemstone," she said, and I thought she might be right. Hejdanatt and I were a bit jealous of her discovery and began searching more carefully among the stones on the shore, but neither of us could find anything like the white jewel.

Before long we realized it was lunchtime, so we climbed up from the river and walked back to the village. My mother and father had returned from work for lunch, and the smell of grilling fish wafted from the house. After promising to continue our adventures in the afternoon, we went our separate ways.

My mother was in the kitchen stirring a pot of soup, while my father sat on the sofa in the living room finishing the newspaper he had started this morning. I decided to interrupt his reading by climbing onto his lap.

Then we waited a long while, stomachs growling with hunger, for Olle to come home from soccer. I suggested we eat without him, but my father said we must wait, so I was forced to simply imagine how delicious the fish and soup and all the rest would taste.

But at last it became apparent that Olle was really much later than usual. What could have happened to him? I would have liked to go look for him at school, but the walk there took more than an hour, which was beyond my strength, especially since I had eaten nothing since morning. I was so weak I doubted I could rise from my chair.

I caught sight of Nulla and the others outside our window. Hejdanatt came to the door and called for me. I barely managed to drag myself over to meet her.

"Let's go," she said. I just shook my head, unable to speak. "Haven't you eaten yet?" she asked.

"No," I told her. "We haven't even started. Olle's not back from school and we have to wait for him."

"He must have stopped off somewhere on the way home," Hejdanatt said.

"I suppose so," I said. But I doubted he'd have lingered long if he were as hungry as I was. He was usually so prompt when it came to meals.

"You should go ahead without me," I told Hejdanatt. "I'll come along once I've eaten. Where do you think you'll be?"

"You know," said Hejdanatt, ignoring my question, "for some reason I think Olle may have gone to the Western Forest. It's right on the way home from school, almost like a shortcut. Maybe he tried to go through."

This thought took my breath away. The Western Forest? Hejdanatt was right that it stood between our village and the school. Our normal route went far out of the way to steer clear of the forest. But there was a path—a narrow and dark one—that went straight through. The grown-ups sometimes took it, and the boys too, as a test of courage if there were several in a group, but we girls never went that way.

Had Olle, in his hurry to get home, gone that way alone? If he had, perhaps the monster we'd heard about had got him! I stood there in the doorway, terrified, even forgetting how hungry I was.

Hejdanatt tried to reassure me, insisting he would be home soon, but I could only shake my head. "If he were coming home, he'd be here by now," I told her. I knew he would never skip a meal if he had a choice. I turned to see my father get up from the kitchen table and go into the living room to telephone the school.

"Is Olle still there?" he asked. Hejdanatt and I watched for any change in his expression. He listened for a moment, gripping the phone tightly. "I see," he said. "Thank you." Then he put down the receiver.

"Is he still playing soccer?" I asked him, but he just shook his head.

"They said practice ended quite some time ago and everyone has gone home." Before these words were out of his mouth, a shiver went through my body. I was sure now that he had taken the road through the forest and that the monster had caught him.

But I wasn't about to tell my mother and father what I was thinking. I knew how much they loved Olle, and if they thought he'd been captured by a monster, cut into pieces, and carried away to some secret spot in the forest, they would have gone mad with grief. I didn't want to cause them such terrible pain.

But what was I to do? The rumors said that the monster cut up the children but didn't kill them right away. Instead he took them deep into the forest to suffer a slow and painful death. Then perhaps Olle was still alive. Perhaps he was hurt but had managed to survive and was hidden away somewhere. If that were so, then I would go to his rescue. He was my big brother after all, and that's what any good sister would do.

"Hejdanatt," I said, taking her by the hand, going outside, and shutting the door, "I think you're right. I think Olle took the forest road and was caught by the monster. I have to try to find him, and I'm hoping you and the others will come with me."

A terrified look spread over Hejdanatt's face. "But we don't even know that the monster got him," she said.

"I can't stay here and do nothing!" I told her. "The monster could be doing horrible things to him even as we speak!" I started to run. I couldn't hold still anymore, and I suppose part of me didn't want Hejdanatt to see the tears welling up in my eyes.

A few moments later, I was hurrying as fast as I could toward the forest, praying for Olle—my dear, naughty brother Olle. Why would you have gone in the monster's lair? I prayed he was alive, that the monster had spared him even if he was in its clutches, and that my trembling legs would carry me to him in time.

I soon found myself near the entrance to the forest. When you had passed along the road from the village through a pleasant grove, you came suddenly to a wall of massive, dark fir trees: the Western Forest. Although it was summertime, there was no sign that animals lived here. In the trees along the way, I had heard birds singing and seen tracks left by all sorts of creatures, but the forest was dark and silent, as though it absorbed all the sound around it.

I was determined to keep going, to run straight on into the wall of trees, knowing that if I stopped or hesitated I might never get my legs moving again. I was close now, the entrance to the forest in sight, but the path ahead, beneath the overhanging limbs, was dark and obscure. Still, I had no choice but to go on.

But just as I was about to pass under the first dark boughs, an old man and woman came walking out of a thicket by the path. I had never laid eyes on either of them before.

"Young lady!" said the old man, beckoning to me. "Please stop. You must not enter the forest."

But I couldn't stop; I couldn't have kept my legs from propelling me forward even if I'd tried. Then, as I ran on, another old man and woman appeared from the underbrush and called out to me as well.

"Don't go into the forest!"

I wanted to tell them I understood, but that my brother was in there and I had to go. But I was so breathless from running that the words just wouldn't come out.

Still a third and then a fourth old couple appeared from different spots near the forest, and all of them tried to stop me, but at last I closed my eyes and ignored them. I was nearly under the trees now. All I had to do was run straight ahead.

Perhaps because my eyes were closed, I could hear everything quite clearly—the sound of my footsteps and my breath and the voices of the old people calling to me. I knew that they were worried, but the voice I wanted to hear was Olle's.

The heat of the sun on my back suddenly vanished, and the warm summer air turned chilly. Though my eyes were still closed, I knew I had entered the forest. And it wasn't just the warmth that was gone—the voices of all the old people, which had been so distinct a moment before, had fallen silent now. The sounds of the outside world could not reach me here. Even the sounds of my own breath and footsteps were muffled and faint. I opened my eyes, needing to be certain I was still running, still breathing.

And indeed I was. When I turned to look back, I could see that I had barely come any distance at all from the first rank of trees. The old people were nowhere to be seen.

Then I came to an abrupt halt. Looking back, I had spotted several figures in a patch of sunlight just beyond the shadows of the trees—Nulla and Inte, if I wasn't mistaken, and Hejdanatt, Adju, and Nej too. All of them running after me.

Though I had wanted their help when I had set out, now that I saw them here I knew it was wrong to let them come with me, wrong to lead them into the clutches of a terrible monster. I would never want any harm to come to them.

I held up my palms to stop them. "Don't come in here!" I called as loudly as I could. But my voice seemed to die as it left my mouth, and what should have been a loud shout came out as barely more than a whisper. In the end, I wasn't sure whether any sound had emerged at all.

I tried shouting again, but again I couldn't even hear my own voice. It was just as I'd imagined—this strange forest was actually sucking up all the sound. The fir trees all around were enormous, and their limbs seemed to reach out for me. Their needles were dark green, shading to pitch black in the shadows below. Anything at all might have been hiding in this gloom—sinister things that would have felt right at home in such an awful spot. The thick roots of the trees made a pattern of deep furrows in the murky forest floor. It was a net cast over the ground, and it reminded me somehow of the net of golden scales I had seen just hours before, glinting on the belly of the river trout. But this one seemed evil, with none of the beauty of the fish.

I knew for sure now that this was no place for my friends!

I turned around to face them, crossed my arms in front of me to signal that they should stop. But they kept coming straight toward me—though apparently unable to see me as they ran. But of course!—until I made my way in here, I hadn't been able to see anything inside either. How could they see me in these deep shadows?

I started back the way I came, but the roots seemed to trip me up and I fell flat on my face. How could this be? Coming in, I'd had no trouble running with my eyes closed, but now that I was trying to go back, the roots heaved up and prevented me from leaving. I had hit my knee in the fall and it hurt a great deal, but just as I was forcing myself to my feet again, Nulla and the others reached the edge of the forest and came rushing in.

"Kerstin!" Hejdanatt called when she caught sight of me. As I'd thought, from outside I must have been invisible, even though I'd stopped just a few steps into the forest. She ran straight to me and gave me a hug. "I'm sorry I didn't want to come with you," she said, almost in tears.

I embraced her for a moment before taking a step back. "No, Hejdanatt," I said. "You shouldn't be here, and neither should the others. This is a terrible place. I want you to go back—all of you. I'll go on alone."

Inte looked at me for a moment, and then when he spoke up he said the oddest thing. "It may be terrible," he said, "but we've already come all this way."

"Don't be silly, Inte. We're barely past the entrance," I said. But when I looked toward the edge of the trees and the patch of sunlight that should have been right beyond, I saw nothing but thick trunks and shadows. Worse still, there was no sign now of the narrow path I had followed into the forest. In its place I saw a thick carpet of dried fir boughs and the undulating web of roots.

A shudder ran through me, and my eyes drifted upward.

But like everything else that had disappeared, the blue summer sky that should have been above our heads was nowhere to be seen. Thick, dark branches crowded in from every direction, lacing together, and though the treetops were obscured somewhere overhead, I knew I had never seen such tall trees before.

As it finally began to dawn on me that we were now deep in the heart of the forest, my body started to tremble. The other girls were shivering too. Nulla and Inte were putting up a brave front, but Inte looked terribly pale even in the dim light. Nej and Adju held hands and looked around timidly.

"Why did you ever come so far into this horrible place all by yourself?" Hejdanatt said. I told them I had gone no farther than the entrance, but clearly they didn't believe me.

"The entrance?" Nulla said. "We ran a long, long way from the entrance before we caught sight of you here, far off the path."

How very odd, I thought. What had happened? How had I come to be here? I had no idea. But one thing was certain: there was something uncanny about this forest, something evil lurking around us.

"We can't worry about that now," I said. "Let's get back to the path."

Everyone agreed immediately, and Nulla led the way. I took Hejdanatt's hand and followed him, and the rest came right behind. But no matter how far Nulla walked, we saw nothing resembling a path.

"It ought to be right around here," Nulla said, his puzzled face swiveling back and forth. But there was no sign of it anywhere.

I knew then what had happened: the forest had hidden the path from us to make certain we stayed lost forever. And I knew, too, that there was a monster here, and that the forest was its ally. As for me, my only allies were these five children.

At this point Nej and Adju began to cry. There were tears in Inte's eyes too, and even Nulla and Hejdanatt seemed to be struggling to keep calm.

I had to be strong, I told myself. I had led my friends in here, and I would find a way to get them out. But if I was going to succeed in this undertaking, I couldn't let myself be beaten by these terrible trees.

"Why don't we sing?" I said, and I started into a song myself.

Die! Die! Die! Die! Every last one of you'll die!
Every last one of you'll die! Die! Time is a-wasting! So die!
You'll never get out of the woods, oh no!
Not one of you'll get home alive!

My friends screamed as the words faded into the shadows, but somehow I wasn't sure what I had just sung.

"What was that?" I murmured. It certainly wasn't the song I had intended to sing, which would have been something bright, something to cheer us up. Then where had this song come from?

Inte burst into tears, and I knew Hejdanatt would be next. In fact, she was tapping me on the shoulder, and when I turned to look, great drops were collecting in her bloodshot eyes. "Why would you want to sing something so horrible?" she said.

"Never mind," said Nulla. "I'll sing."

Now the fun begins, my dears!
One of you shortly will die!
It's up to you to choose just who,
But one of you shortly must die!
So pick the one who's not much fun!
Since one of you shortly must die!

Another scream met Nulla's song, but this time I was screaming too.

"Stop!" I yelled, but one look at his pale face told me that he'd had no more control over the lyrics than I'd had. Those were not the words he'd wanted to sing.

Just then Adju called Nej's name and reached out to hold her, but Nej's body floated lightly away, up in the air.

As she was lofted up, Nej screamed, and the rest of us answered with a piercing cry. We watched, stunned, as she floated up among the branches, paused for a moment, then spun around and flew off into the depths of the forest.

"Nej!" Nulla called, beginning to run after her as she disappeared into the trees. The rest of us followed.

But she was flying too fast and we couldn't keep up. Her screams faded into the distance as we lost sight of her.

"Neeeeej!" Nulla called again, but she was gone.

So who'll be next? Who's next to die?
Whoever it is won't simply fly.
This time'll be slower, with lots more pain!
You'll suffer and suffer, then you'll perish in vain!

It was Adju's turn to offer a tune, though she clearly had no more idea what she was singing than we'd had. Tears were running down her face, and perhaps she had simply opened her mouth to weep aloud and this hideous song came out.

Inte begged her to stop, but as the song came to an end she floated up into the air just as Nej had a moment ago. She let out a horrible scream and then, right before our eyes, the little bare legs dangling below Adju's skirt were snapped off at the knees. Blood spurted out, drenching us as we stood looking up at her, and we scattered, our mouths gaping open in horror.

Adju's body drifted up. We heard a few whimpering sounds and then it, too, soared off into the forest. This time, though, no one made a move to follow.

A plopping sound echoed behind us, and we turned to see Adju's severed legs settling to earth; but strangely, horribly, they landed on their feet and stood planted together as though Adju were still with them. Then they began to run toward us.

We scattered again, terrified, but the legs seemed to have no interest in us, running straight past and into the forest in the same direction her body had gone. Clip, clop, clip, clop, clip, clop...until they vanished from sight.

We stood there stunned, unable to take in what was happening. I knew only that I deeply regretted having come into this forest. I was all but certain I would never see Olle again, and now Nej and

Adju were gone too. And I had no idea how the rest of us would ever get out.

Hejdanatt stood next to me, clutching my hand and trembling. All at once her mouth opened as though she were about to say something. No! I thought. But it was too late.

> *The next one to go will suffer still more!*
> *The next will suffer a lot!*
> *You'll pray to die faster, but faster's a bore,*
> *Get ready to suffer, to suffer still more!*

I looked at Nulla and Inte, and they looked back at me. Inte's mouth opened as though to beg for help, but nothing came out. Then he spat out a single word: "Me!"

Yet nothing happened to him.

"You have to say a name," Nulla said.

"Quiet, Nulla!" Inte said, but before our minds could even register what he'd done, Nulla floated into the air. We heard him yell "No!" as he sailed high up among the fir branches. Then, as he paused a moment directly above us, both arms and both legs were torn from his body; and before he could even scream, what was left of him shot away through the trees. The arms and legs fell to earth and went chasing after.

We stood staring, unable even to breathe.

Hejdanatt's eyes were closed and her body had gone rigid. Inte's expression was blank and he was shaking uncontrollably, but he struggled to his feet, sobbed aloud for a moment, and then very quietly said his own name. "Inte."

Instantly he rose up in the air and his arms and legs came away from his body. His torso gave a violent twist and ripped apart at the waist, spilling out his blood and the full length of his intestines onto the earth below. Plop, plop, plop! When they were emptied out, his head and torso sailed off into the forest, and his arms and legs followed after on the ground.

That left just Hejdanatt and me. She was weeping loudly, but I got her attention and put my finger to my lips to signal that we should keep quiet. Our voices were clearly not our own here in the forest, so the only thing we could do was stop using them.

Soon she fell silent. I nodded to her and then started to walk in the opposite direction from the point where our friends had disappeared. Hejdanatt, clutching my hand, followed close behind.

The forest floor was rough and made for hard going. The roots and branches and fallen twigs seemed to grasp at our feet and do everything they could to prevent us from making progress.

Then, before we had gone very far at all, Hejdanatt stepped on a dried branch, and the cracking sound seemed to become a voice, saying:

Well then…

Startled, we stopped short. I was on the point of crying out, and I could only imagine that Hejdanatt was too. She put her hand up to cover her mouth, and carefully lifted her foot from the branch. Instead of another crunch, we heard:

Who's next?

Whatever it was—the monster or this horrible forest itself—it seemed to have control of every possible sound.

Hejdanatt shook her head back and forth and then started to run, her hand still clasped to her mouth. Each twig she stepped on, each pebble she dislodged, each branch she pushed out of the way made a slight sound, and I soon understood that together they had become a new song.

> *Well then, who's next?*
> *Well then, who's next?*
> *Well then, who'll be the next one to die?*
> *Who would be best?*
> *And what should you do?*
> *Yes, what should you do?*
> *Since the last one to go*
> *Will be suffering for two!*

It was the most horrible song yet. But if we held our tongues, if we did not say any more names, we should be safe. I put my hand over my mouth and ran off after Hejdanatt—but the sounds my feet made began singing too, a whole medley of gruesome songs.

> *The last will be worst, that's all that I'll say.*
> *The last will feel pain that won't go away.*
> *So sooner is better, if only a bit.*
> *The last one will suffer until I see fit.*

> *So die, die, die, die, each one of you die!*
> *Now, now, now, now, each one of you now!*
> *So run, run, run, run, as fast as you can.*
> *You won't get away, that's all that I'll say.*
> *Your doom is all part of my plan!*

> *Where are you going, my sweet little girls?*
> *Where do you think you can flee?*
> *Why are you running and where will you go?*

You'll never, no never, flee me!

The faster you run, the more it will hurt!
The pain will run faster than you!
The pain, oh the pain, oh the pain, pain, pain, pain!
Only your pain will seem true!

We ran in a straight line, our jaws clenched tight, but there was no sign of the entrance or even the path we had followed in. At last, however, when we had run a long way in utter silence, we caught sight of a glimmer of light beyond the trees: the end of the forest!

We'd done it!

We ran on, steering toward the light. At the thought that we were seeing the sun again after all this time, the tears I had been holding back came pouring out. Gradually the light began to grow. The entrance was near now! But then Hejdanatt, who had run a bit ahead, fell to the ground, and the sound of her fall turned into a single line of song.

Away, away, away, away, you must stop running away!

She looked even more terrified than before, but she pulled herself to her feet and followed me as I dashed on ahead. It was all we could do to avoid the roots and dead branches on the ground, and the branches striking us in the face, but we ran on.

The entrance was near now, and we could see the countryside beyond. We suddenly realized that we had found the path again, and that a little way ahead it was lit by the sun, lined with green grass!

Just a little farther now!

But at that moment I remembered the odd thing that had

happened when I was here before, how I'd thought I was barely inside when in fact, by the time my friends had found me, I was somehow deep in the forest. It wasn't just sound that was beyond our control among these strange trees—space itself seemed to be manipulated by someone or something else. So, I suddenly found myself wondering, was that really the entrance, really the sun shining brightly just a little way ahead?

I stopped and reached out to take hold of Hejdanatt as she raced by me. But I missed her hand and she ran past, dashing for the light. As she ran, each footstep was singing.

Die! Die! Die! Die! Die! Die! Die! Die!

Perhaps because this song was ringing in her ears, she didn't seem to notice that I was no longer running. I took one more step to follow her, but that too became a song.

How clever of you to see!

So I'd been right! As I watched, Hejdanatt reached the edge of the forest. I tried calling to her, but her name died in my throat. Hejdanatt! But the cry never left my lips. Hejdanatt!

She took a single step out into the sun, her skin glowing in the brilliant light. She ran a few steps farther over the bright green grass. Then she turned to look back, her face radiant with joy. It certainly seemed as though she had managed to escape the forest.

But then that momentary look of delight faded, and I knew my worst fears were justified. The sunlight flooding down on her was extinguished in an instant, and the field of green vanished. The shadows closed in around her, and what should have been the bright world beyond became the dark depths of the forest itself.

In reality, she had never left at all—this horrible forest had simply allowed her to think she had, for the briefest of moments. Her head spun this way and that as she fought to understand what was happening, and then she looked back at me.

The look of horror on that face made my hair stand on end. Her hand, which had been clutched to her mouth, fell limp at her side, and her eyes rolled back in her head. Her lips parted and I caught a glimpse of her tongue lolled at the back of her throat. Blood dripping from her nostrils traced lines down her cheeks. Her eyes got terribly wide and her hands reached up to close around her throat. And then she began to repeat her own name over and over. "Hejdanatt, Hejdanatt, Hejdanatt, Hejdanatt."

Even after she floated up among the branches, she continued to say it. "Hejdanatt, Hejdanatt..." But when her arms and legs had been torn away, her torso ripped in two, her neck spun violently and her head twisted off, she at last fell silent.

The head sailed away to the center of the forest, and the rest of her, having fallen to the ground, reformed itself—two arms, two legs, hips, and torso—to follow. But I was quicker; I fell upon the pieces and held them fast.

I'd realized I wouldn't be able to get out of the forest. It had let us hope we could escape, only to draw us back in. There was no reason to think it would ever let me out. So I gave up. I would go to look for Olle instead; I owed that much to my dear brother.

But where to find him? It seemed logical that he would be where the bodies of the others had gone, where the severed pieces had gathered to rejoin the flying heads and torsos.

I jumped on Hejdanatt's back, where it floated between her arms and legs. It was a ghastly place to sit, with blood oozing from the severed neck and arms and waist, but I had no other options. My own legs could never keep up with her head, but as I knew all too well, these pieces of her body would move through the forest with amazing speed.

Clutching my gruesome mount, I sped deep into the heart of the forest. The green grew darker and darker until it was almost pitch black, until the forest itself became an impenetrable shadow. The limbs of the fir trees were piled up above me, and all trace of the sky and sunlight had vanished. There were no animals, no birds or insects, nor even any plants other than the firs—these trees that seemed to have such a seething hatred for children. There were no more voices here, no sound at all.

How deep could the forest be? How far was I going? Outside, the sun would be shining, the day still warm, but around me all was darkness. I could no longer distinguish one tree from another. Hejdanatt's headless body seemed to know the way though.

But then as we rushed on through the forest, the silence was broken, the patter of Hejdanatt's hands and feet turning into a new song.

The last one, the last, but you get the best!
You'll suffer the most, hurt more than the rest!
More pain and more sorrow, more suffering and sting,
But slowly, so slowly, you'll die—that's the thing!
The last one, the last, the last one to go!
But what is your name? I'm anxious to know!
So tell me, do tell me, and then if you will,
I'll wait just a moment, be slow to the kill!
And even the pain—I may make it less.
But still in the end, you'll die like the rest.
I'll kill you, I'll kill you, the last one to go!
I'll kill you, I'll kill you, though ever so slow!
Your legs and your arms and your head I'll pluck out.

Your guts will come tumbling, will pour from the spout!
So slowly, so slowly, I'll watch as you perish!
Laughing and dancing—the moment I'll cherish!
So pleasant! So painful! I'll watch as you die!
So die, die, die, die, die, die, DIE!

With my hands holding tight to Hejdanatt's shoulders, I couldn't cover my ears. I thought about trying to block out the song with my own voice, but I had no idea what would come out of my mouth. I could only clench my teeth and listen.

For a long time, Hejdanatt's body ran straight ahead, deeper into the forest, but then it abruptly began to veer off, making a long, gradual curve to the right. Eventually I realized that Hejdanatt—or what was left of her—was making clockwise circuits. One lap...two. And still she ran on. Three, then four laps, but as we were beginning the fifth, I began to see that the circle was slowly shrinking in diameter. The trees we had passed on the inside the last time around were now moving past us on the outside. The body was tracing a great vortex—but what was waiting for me at the center?

I squinted toward the spot where our spiral was converging, where my ride would end, but it was still a good way off, and I couldn't see for the trees. Hejdanatt's footsteps—and handsteps—were repeating the same word over and over now.

Die, die, die, die, die, die, die, die, die, die, die, die!

The circles were growing tighter and faster, and so at last I jumped from the headless back. I hit the ground and rolled for a few yards until I struck a tree trunk. The blow sent a wave of pain through my shoulder, but I couldn't cry out, couldn't even groan.

Ignoring my injury as best I could, I scrambled to my feet and began walking toward the center of the dark spiral Hejdanatt's body had been tracing. It was so murky that I couldn't even see to avoid the fir branches, which struck me in the face again and again, but I soon learned to move slowly, holding both hands out in front of me.

Die! Die! Die! Die! Die! Die! Die! Die! Die! Die! Die!

Hejdanatt's racing steps—and the song with them—passed behind me and receded to the far side of the circle. I ignored them and walked on.

Every time my foot tread on a dried branch or struck a root, my heart skipped a beat. I had the terrible feeling I might be stepping on Nulla or Inte, Adju or Nej, whose bodies had flown here to the heart of the forest. If that happened, I was sure I wouldn't be able to keep myself from screaming or from begging forgiveness from the body of my dead friend. But just as surely, if I did, my voice would turn into my own name and I would suffer that slow, painful death that the song of Hejdanatt's footsteps had promised.

My whole body was trembling, but I kept on my course to the center of the spiral. I knew somehow that I had to see whatever it was that I would find there; and, too, I was all but certain I would find Olle, most likely in the same state as the others—arms and legs and even head ripped from his body. The prospect was frightening, and I was sure I'd scream—and immediately suffer a fate like Olle's or perhaps still worse.

But what did it matter? I'd come here to find him, and if I could just manage to do that, then I didn't care what happened afterwards.

Suddenly I was brought up short. What was that? In the distance, among all the enormous fir trees, in exactly the spot for which I was heading, I could make out a more slender tree that appeared to be moving in an odd fashion. The limbs were swaying back and forth, up and down, quite at random, while the trunk twisted around and around.

But I quickly realized it wasn't a fir tree at all.

It was so dark that I couldn't be sure until I was very close, but it clearly was not a tree. It looked like a person—a very oddly shaped person. Or perhaps "person" wasn't the right word. It had a single torso, from which a great many arms were growing, and both the torso and the legs below were extremely long and thin. It appeared as though the legs had been cobbled together by taking the severed sections of many different legs and stacking them one on top of the other; and the torso, too, consisted of lots of trunks and hips piled together to achieve this great length, this one elongated body.

The body and arms resembled an enormous, upright, disgusting centipede, but when you added the long legs it took on human form. What's more, there was a head on top of all this.

But when I looked up at it, I nearly fainted before I could even scream. The head, like the rest of the creature, consisted of many different heads all mashed together, each one with a face looking out, and on each face was a different expression.

My body froze with terror.

Surely this must be the Monster of the Forest. And yet its body appeared to have been made from the bodies of my friends.

My horror came from this realization, the knowledge that Nulla and Inte and Adju and Nej were somewhere in there, that their heads were all part of the monster's head—and perhaps most of all from the thought that I was now willing to join them as well. I somehow instantly felt it would be easier to become a part of the monster than it was to remain out here, alone and terrified.

But that wasn't true! Surely Nulla and the others hadn't gone happily to their fate. As my eyes wandered from one face to another, I could see that nearly all of them were twisted with pain. The monster must have taken the children into its body and was now slowly killing them. Slowly, painfully, gradually killing them.

No! I couldn't let it catch me! I made a decision: I would bring the monster down instead. I would save those children—my friends!—suffering there inside.

But how? I was just a young girl with no weapons. Not to mention the fact that I was petrified with fear, almost unable to breathe. What could I possibly do?

I hadn't the faintest idea.

My own impotence made we want to cry. Everyone in the village and at school had always told me how steady and reliable I was—and I'd even come to think of myself that way. But here in this forest, face to face with this monster, I had come to realize that I was just a child like the others, foolish and powerless and destined to die.

Die! Die! Die! Die! Die! Die! Die! Die! Die! Die! Die!

Hejdanatt's body passed behind me again. It wouldn't be long before it reached the monster and Hejdanatt, too, would join the others. But as I watched her pass, I suddenly heard a voice behind me.

"Kerstin!"

Someone was calling my name.

"Kerstin!"

I turned to look at the monster and saw Hejdanatt's pale face there in the midst of the others. The lines of blood had dried on her cheeks, and she was staring straight at me.

"Kerstin!"

I wanted to call back, to tell her I was here, but I was too frightened.

"Kerstin! Get on my body!" she cried.

I hesitated. Why did she want me to get back on? And how could I? She was running too fast.

But she called again. "Kerstin! Get on!" And this time it was just as her body was passing me.

Die! Die! Die! Die! Die! Die! Die! Die! Die! Die! Die!

It was impossible—my arms and legs were frozen with fear.

"Don't give up, Kerstin!"

Another voice was calling. I looked back at the monster and could see Nulla's face right near Hejdanatt's.

"Kerstin! Get on Hejdanatt's body!" Inte was there too.

"Kerstin!" "Kerstin!" Adju and Nej as well.

"Now!"

So I did what I'd thought was impossible: I jumped on her back as it charged by.

Die! Die! Die! Die! Die! Die! Die! Die! Die!

I clung on desperately to keep from being thrown as we raced at breakneck speed, my eyes fixed on the monster at the center of our ever-tightening circles. I could feel tears welling up in my eyes. My dear, dear friends were there, inside that hateful beast, and the body of my sweet Hejdanatt would soon be part of it too.

At the end of a few more laps, we finally arrived at the monster's feet. I had no idea what would happen now, but I steeled myself as I clung to Hejdanatt's back.

"Come!"

Hejdanatt's voice was calling from above. And with that, her body jumped onto the monster's leg and began clambering up. I was doing my best to stay on, but without a head there was little to cling to and I felt myself slipping off.

"Hold on, Kerstin!" Hejdanatt's head called.

I wrapped my arms around her waist and held on for dear life. When we had climbed to the monster's body, a great many hands came reaching toward me. I wanted to cry out, but just as one hand was about to grab me another one appeared to fend it off.

"Don't worry, Kerstin! I'll protect you!" It was Inte's voice, and it must have been his hand that had defended me just now.

"I will too!" This was Nulla, calling from above, and this time when another hand reached out to take hold of me, there were two hands to brush it away. With their help, Hejdanatt's body was able to reach the top of the monster's torso. When we had climbed above the spot where Nulla's and Inte's hands were attached, we came to Adju's and Nej's, and they helped us in the same way.

Thank you, Adju! Thank you, Nej!

I still had no idea what I was going to do, but I was somehow sure I was doing what I had to do. I knew, of course, because my dear friends thought it was important enough to be helping me like this.

Dodging the last of the grasping arms, Hejdanatt's body leapt up and held fast to the enormous head. Then, using the children's mouths and nostrils as finger- and toeholds, it continued to climb.

"Kerstin, thank you!"

"Just a little farther, Kerstin!"

"Kerstin!"

"Kerstin!"

As I clung to Hejdanatt's back, we passed very near her face, as well as Nulla's, Inte's, Adju's, and Nej's, but as I leaned over to give each of them a kiss, we reached the top of the monster's head.

Though the view from this height was dizzying, when I looked up, the branches of the evil trees still loomed high over us and the canopy of the forest was far above.

But what should I do now? How was I going to bring down the monster?

"Kerstin!"

This time it was a new voice, a familiar voice! I climbed off of Hejdanatt's back and stood on top of the head. At my feet was Olle's face! My dear brother!

"Olle!" I was about to cry out, but I held my tongue.

"Don't cry, Kerstin! You mustn't cry!"

But how can I not? I wanted to ask him.

Olle's pain and suffering were written on his face. It was hard to believe that it was the same Olle, the boy who was always so quick to laugh, who always had a joke at the ready.

"Kerstin, you have to get inside the monster's head now," he said, though I had no idea what that could mean or how I would accomplish it. "Quickly, get inside the head and swallow the monster!"

Inside? Swallow the monster? If I got inside its head, wouldn't that mean it was eating me rather than the other way around? I stood there crying and shaking my head in confusion until Olle spoke up again.

"Don't worry, Kerstin," he said. "When you get into his head, you'll be able to swallow him up."

It still made no sense. How was I going to eat this monster?

"Kerstin!"

I needed desperately to ask how to do what he was asking, but I knew just as well that I had to keep quiet. What a horrible fate for a girl like me to be unable to speak!

But at last I got control of myself, wiped away my tears, and mouthed my question to Olle's face.

How?

"Like this!" he said, and then he opened his mouth as wide as he could. At almost the same instant, Hejdanatt's body, which had been waiting behind me, jumped up and pressed my head down into Olle's gaping mouth.

His face, lodged there at the very top of the monster's head, ate me up and swallowed me down.

Round-and-Round Devil

I'M STARVED. 7-Eleven's a long way off. La di da di da da da...

"Hey, old woman, got anything to eat?"

«Hungry? I'll make you something.»

"*Make* me something?—I'm hungry *now*!"

«Patience, patience. Let's see what we have.»

"Well, be quick about it! I'll beat the shit out of you if you dawdle around, fucking old woman."

«Patience, patience...»

"So where is it?"

«I'm afraid we're out of rice.»

"Who gives a fuck what we're out of! Where's my grub?"

«I'm sorry, but you...»

"Don't call me 'you'! It's 'Mr. Hideo,' bitch."

«I'm sorry, Mr. Hideo.»

"Are you making fun of me?" I'll post it on Voice of Heaven, bitch! "You're a fucking housewife! It's your *job* to make my dinner!"

Who needs people who can't pull their weight? I'll turn you into an animal—like the parents turned into pigs in *Spirited Away*. My mom, the fat pig.

And she clams up the minute I say anything—now that's just fucked. Fucking annoying's what she is! Can't stand all her tiptoeing around. Die, you fat pig!

"Hey, you! Get your ass moving or I'll kill you. All you do is stuff your face, then there's nothing for me, nothing for Mr. Hideo to eat!"

«I'm so sorry.»

"Shit! So go out and *get* something! Curry—that's what I want, nice and spicy. If you're not back in ten seconds, I'll take it out of your hide. I'll beat the crap out of you, an extra socko for every second over ten."

«No, please.»

"No whining! On your mark, get set, *go*!"

«Wait...»

"One, two..."

Get busy, you fucking pig! Or fuck off and die! Better yet, get me some curry and then fuck off and die!

"Five, six..."

Useless fucking pig!

"Nine, ten!"

One ass-kicking coming right up! La di da di DA!

Whoa! Ashtray landed right back o' the bitch's head! Ash and shit *every*where! Least it got her out the fuckin' door. Bitch don't even know she's a woman anymore. Fuckin' worst-case *scenario*! Regular fucking Cinderella. Something fucked about that: "My mom's Cinderella." Fucking crazy, that is.

And I'm *still* hungry as hell.

A true royal bitch pain. Must at least be some cup ramen round here somewhere.

Fuck me! Not one! Fucking *unbelievable!* Something weirdly fucked about a house doesn't have even *one* fucking cup ramen. *Fucking* unbelievable.

Curry? Maybe I should've told her to get something else.

Cup noodles! Shit, now I want cup noodles! Still…curry…? Probably better for you anyway.

But *shit* I'm hungry!

Shit, I'm so fucking hungry I'd eat *any* fuckin' thing at this point.

Ping!

Better check Voice of Heaven.

La di da di da di da di la di da di da di da. La di shit-for-brains di da di da di da.

Lots of new shit!

God's Court now in session. Defendant: Round-and-Round Devil. Day Five.

God's watching. The Round-and-Round Devil used to kill little kitties & puppies. Now he kills people. So the verdict is the death penalty.

God has spoken. Kill yourself now!

Clueless assholes.

The whole Chofu Armageddon was pointless.

No, it had a perfectly good point: it was a fucking lot of fun. Fucking lot of fun to watch from a safe distance while a bunch of assholes beat the shit out of each other.

Five middle school kids were killed in the Armageddon, but turns out they were all innocent—no Round-and-Round among them. Now God's guilty instead. God should die too.

Don't worry, he's dying.

If there were a real God, he would never have let
Armageddon happen—or let the Round-and-Round Devil
live.
The Round-and-Round Devil is the new God!

Right you are! I *am* the new God! Heh heh heh hi hi!

Log on, Monster Man. What have you got to say for
yourself?

Nothing quite yet. Be patient.

I'm busy cutting up Child Four, no time to post.
And planning for Child Five, and Six. Busy, busy. A
monster's work is never done. I'd love to follow V of
H but I don't have time now.☹

Oh, I'm following all right, you fake fuck.

And you can bet I'd do Four and Five if could find them here
in Chofu. Who doesn't like a challenge? You bet your ass I'd do
them. But you really can't improvise when it comes to killing kids.
Rush things and it gets all fucked up. Still, it leaves a bad taste in
your mouth, ending like that with the one still alive. I just need
one more chance.

But probably not right now. Looks like Armageddon's over,
so no cover—and another body would stir things up, get them
searching house to house. Way too risky.

But fuck, what to do about all this *nervous energy*?

La di da di da di da...

Shit! I'm hungry. Where the fuck is that woman?

Maybe I should post after all, something like: Live from the
Yoshiba funeral, victims of the Round-and-Round. Namu
Amida Butsu, Namu Amida Butsu.

Better I say the prayers than some idiot priest. *Achieve* nirvana,
and that's an *order*! Can't quite believe the husband died too. But
it's "his funeral," as they say. A damn shame, but I suppose if

you're the kind's going to commit suicide, you'll do it eventually no matter what else happens. Just hope he doesn't end up putting a hex on me. This is a *no-curse zone*, thank you very much!

Nanmaidabuu, Nanmaidabuu. Shit.

I'm SO hungry I can't fucking *stand* it!

FUCK the old lady!

Death to fucking old ladies! Death! Death! Death!

Pork cutlet cur-ry, poooork cutlet cur-ry, pooooork cutlet cur-ry, hip hip hooray! Lot of good it does me to cheer—I still haven't got any. Go, pork cutlet cur-ry! Get a hit!

Curry, curry, curry, curry! Cuuuuurry, curry. Hot curry!

Fuck.

Wha? Back at last, you dumb bitch? Trying to starve me to death?

Curry, curry, curry, curry!

What the fuck? That's just the shit you get at the convenience store.

"What the fuck is that? I told you to get pork cutlet curry and you come back with this shit."

«What? Oh dear, you're right. I'm sorry. I'll go back and change it for the right kind.»

"Don't be an idiot. Hand it over. I'll eat this while you go back and get the pork cutlet curry."

«Oh dear, can you really eat that much?»

"Can I really eat that much? I'm fucking *starved*, bitch."

«All right then, I understand. You don't have to shout.»

"Will you shut the *fuck* up? You haven't heard shit if you think that's shouting. Uuuwwwaaaaaaah! Kkkkyyaaaaaaaah!"

«All right, Mr. Hideo. Please calm down!»

"Shut up, bitch! Just go get the curry…But wait a second…don't move…don't go anywhere…hold still…There it is, by the door, some glass broke. There…okay, here we *go*! Kapow! My Galactic Phantom Kick for the little lady who fucked up the curry buy!"

Whoaaa bitch! There you go! Little fragile, aren't we? Anything broken? Maybe you ought to be taking calcium. Or not. Whatever. Get the calcium and die for all I care. But *after* you get me the cutlet curry.

Shit I'm hungry. Curry, curry, curry, curry. Curry burry, furry.

Whoaaah! Not bad! In fact, fucking *deee*licious! Worth waiting for even without the cutlet. But I guess everything tastes good when you're this hungry. Hunger's the best seasoning.

Yum yum *yum*!

Don't think there's enough.

What the?…all gone! Heh? That really wasn't enough. My stomach's still empty—glad I told the old bag to get the cutlet curry.

So here I am, just sitting around, looking forward to my cutlet curry. Cutlet, cutlet, cutlet, cutlet…curry! Fufufufufufufufufufu fufufuuuufu!

The Round-and-Round Devil would very much like some curry, if you would be so kind. Guru, guru, boil and bubble, guru, guru *curry*! So you shake it to the right, and you shake it to the left! Spin it all around, Round-and-Round, one, two, and three, Round-and-Round, *spin!*

Ahhh. Oh well, guess I got full waiting for the bitch to come back. But that means a little extra penalty for the old lady, another Round-and-Round Kick!

Ah! She's back. Shit, she's slow. But nothing a little time in the penalty box won't fix. World o' Hurt.

"Hey! Old lady! You're late."

«I'm sorry. They didn't have cutlet curry at the 7-Eleven down the street.»

"Then you should have *run* all the way to where they *did* have it. Looks to me like you've been out for a *walk*! Anyway, don't just stand there and look stupid, hand it over! Then stand over there... and look stupid."

Oops, still haven't choreographed my Round-and-Round Kick. Oh well.

"Take this, bitch!"

Whoa! More blood from the old bitch's head. Whatever.

How 'bout that cutlet curry?

Shit, that's *good*! But can't finish it.

Guess I'll leave some for later.

Ah, I'm full. That's enough.

Okay then, what next? Can't stay shut up in here all the time like those *shut-in* shitheads. Must be some manga or something hitting the stands today.

Ah, yes! The Yoshiba guy's funeral. An *excellent* plan!

I'll go and pay my respects.

Well, not "respects" exactly. More like "*last* respects," except I didn't respect 'em much. But whatever. I'll just go have a look.

"Yo! Heh! Your Hagness! Where's the getup I wore when Grampa died?"

«What?...Oh, yes...we've still got it. Where are you going?»

"Where else *would* I be going in that thing? To a funeral—fu-ne-*ral*!—you idiot!"

«The Yoshiba funeral? Did you have something to do with that?»

"Of course not. I'm just going to have a look."

«You don't just go have a look at a funeral.»

"Shut your trap, Mommy Dearest, or I'll be going to have a look at your funeral."

«Have you got the offering?»

"Offering? What the fuck?"

«When you go to a funeral, you have to take an offering.»

"You mean like your own incense or something?"

«No, no. Don't you know anything? An offering of money, to help with the expenses.»

"Pfft!"

«Do you have any money?»

"Not a yen. But I'm sure you can fix that."

«All right, hold on a minute.»

"So how much are you supposed to give?"

«I'm not sure. I suppose about five thousand yen.»

"Serious? Seems pretty steep."

«Yes, but funerals are expensive.»

"A whole lot of people came when Grampa died. If they all forked over five thousand, you made out like a bandit."

«But most of it went for the expenses.»

Shit! Now *there's* a plan! Stick it to my aunt and her family, send them all off to meet their Buddha, and abscond with the funeral offerings. Might even be able to pin the whole thing on foreigners if I played it right.

Why would anybody *Japanese* kill an entire family? It had to be outsiders. They always jump to conclusions. Why would any adult kill cats and dogs and little kids? It had to be another kid. Must be a *middle school* kid, in fact. Bunch of one-track minds. I guess that Sakakibara thing where that kid killed those other kids, and that other kid in Tottori who killed three whole families—guess those had a big effect on people. Still…

«Here's the money. I put it in the right kind of envelope.»

"Will you look at that?"

«And the suit's upstairs, in the closet in Grampa's old room.»

"Got it. Thanks."

You gotta be kidding me—she really did put five thousand in here. Think I'll just subtract three—no, four.

Whoa! This old suit stinks! Can't go around smelling like mothballs. Old lady needs to get some of those new odorless ones...

If it's going to be that much of a pain, maybe I won't even go.

The Round-and-Round Devil regrets to inform you he will not be attending...

Babbabbarabba! Goronnbo!

Babbabbarabba! Hidenbo!

Tales of Detective Hidenbo, Chapter Three: Hidenbo Goes to the Funeral. *Sure is hot, isn't it, Detective Hidenbo?* You can say that again, Officer Turd. *This black suit's gonna be pretty uncomfortable on a day like this.* You can say that again. *Who even wants to go to a funeral in this heat?* But I don't see how we can come right out and say that, can we, Detective? *I suppose not, but that doesn't change the fact I'd rather be sipping ice coffee in some café.* I'm with you there, Detective, but you can't sound quite so selfish. You can have all the ice coffee you want afterward. *No foolin'?* No foolin.' *Nice and icy?* All the ice you want, ice *cream* for all I care. *Just as long as it's cold. I love it cold.* Is that right? *To tell the truth, my cock's pretty cold, leastwise it's always givin' the cold shoulder to some dame or another.* What are you talking about? *Hot's better than cold when it comes to cocks.* Really? *Then could you use that warm mouth of yours to heat up my cold cock, Hidenbo?* Ughhhhh! He he he! Hold on!

Whoa! That's a whole lot of police. I get it though—they just got through Armageddon but they're worried the V of H guys are going to show up—but they never will now, not with this many cops.

Yoshiba Funeral ☞

Whoa! Will you look at this crowd! Too many mourners, man! But at least I won't stand out. And it would never occur to any of them that Mr. Round-and-Round would show up here. Hee hee.

Ah, here we are.

I guess you're supposed to bow.

And say something like "I'm very sorry for your loss." Sounds right.

"I'm very sorry for your loss." Bow and…bow.

«Would you please sign the guest book?»

Hideo Ozaki, Chofu City, Chofugaoka. I suppose they'd get all bent out of shape if I signed as the Round-and-Round Devil. Bet they'd beat me to a pulp even if I told them it was only a joke. Pretty scary spot for little old me. Yea, though I walk through the valley…and all that. Still, it's kind of interesting at the same time. What would happen if I wrote my name and made a run for it? I could probably get away…Nah, maybe not. They'd probably get me. Reporters snapping my picture, and all these cops…Think I'll just leave my little envelope and go.

Sure is a lot fancier than Grampa's funeral. They must be getting a lot of offerings, but then I suppose it costs every yen of it to put on a spread like this. Bet the media's paying something for the rights to the story. They pay for any old interview these days— probably a pretty good racket. You could even sell souvenirs to a mob like this—"Step right up! Get your Yoshiba Funeral Coffee Mugs! Right over here!" Bunch of fucking hypocrites, every last one of them—and the ones pretending to cry are the worst bastards. Why should they be crying? *They* aren't dead, Yoshiba is—and that's no skin off *their* noses. Why should they be *soooo* sad? And why should so many of them have turned out for this little get-together? I doubt they saw much of Yoshiba before he kicked the bucket. Maybe passed him once or twice a week in the street—at *most*. Some of these suckers didn't see him once a *year*, I bet. Some of them probably hadn't seen him since high school! So why should they be so bent out of shape knowing they'll never see him again? The family—they're the only ones who're really sad, and they're probably mostly wondering what they're going to do now that the breadwinner's gone and abandoned them. Wondering how long they can get by on the money in all those little loot bags. Oops, I mean offering envelopes. I'm not used to the lingo. Well, I hate to tell you, but there's only a thousand yen in mine—though I'm sure it holds five thousand yen worth of sympathy...

Oh, there's his wife. Now *she* can cry all she wants—she's no hypocrite. You've got *real* problems, honey. Not much fun from now on, I have to admit. Still, with both your kids and your husband gone, you're pretty much free to do whatever you want. Maybe tuck in at some all-you-can-eat smorgasbord of sucking off strange men.

But now that you mention it, men really are—

Yoji.

What? What the fuck? Who said that? Someone said something right behind me.

Sounded like a woman saying "Yoji" or something. But there's nobody back there. What the—I must be hearing things. Shit! Don't think I ever—

Yoji.

Whoa, not again! What the fuck's going on? That time I'm *sure* no one was anywhere close. Who is that?

Shit! Must be some sort of auditory hallucination. This is *totally* fucked! The Round-and-Round Devil does *not* have auditory hallucinations!

Maybe it's a ghost? But I haven't killed any women, just those three little kids—and I suppose you could count Yoshiba, but he did it for me himself. So why should a woman be haunting me? Shit, have I got a split personality or something? A woman hiding in my brain? I know I play around with that shit

Yoji. I'm here. Over here. I said I'm over here, Yoji.

"Who *is* that? Who's 'Yoji'?"

I'm Hideo.

Oops, now some guy's looking over this way. That guy standing next to Mrs. Yoshiba. Who is that? Probably a nephew or something. Or some young guy she's banging already. Doesn't matter—but he sure is staring this way. At me.

Shit! Now he's coming over. What do you want, asshole? Keep away or I'll kill you too. Don't come over here. Don't even think about it. Shit, he's really coming.

«Can I help you with something?»

Yoji.

"Yaaaa!"

«Are you okay? Is something wrong?»

Yoji. It's me.

"But who the hell is 'Yoji'?!"

«Please keep your voice down! I'm Yoji Kaneda. Are you feeling sick? Why don't you sit down over here?»

"What? Oh, okay."

So *this* is Yoji.

Yoji.

What?! Do I know this guy?

"Do I know you?"

«I'm not sure. Could you tell me your name?»

Tell him my name?

"No."

This is getting spooky. Time to split.

Yoji.

What?! Now there's another weird guy coming over. Some sort of nerd.

«Wait, please.»

"What do you want?"

Creepy guy! Why is he looking at me like that? Is he gay or something? Wants to suck me off? Or me to suck him?

«Aha ha ha ha ha! What are you doing here?»

What's he laughing at? What a *creep*! I don't get it. Does he know who I am? Who is *he*? Shaggy-haired fatso!

"Who are you?"

«Oh, I'm sorry, I didn't introduce myself. My name is Tansetsu Sakurazuki.»

Tansetsu Sakurazuki? What kind of name is that? Sounds like a character in a late-night anime or some romance novel.

Ah! Tansetsu Sakurazuki! Now I remember!

What do you mean you remember? I've never met the guy.

«So you're here, are you? I thought you'd run off somewhere. Yoji and I were terribly worried. But we're glad we found you. And I must apologize for that strange voice I assume you're hearing inside your head.»

Fucking right I'm hearing it! What the *fuck*?!

"What's going on here?"

«I'm not sure you'll be able to grasp the situation, hearing about it like this out of the blue, but a certain girl we know has gotten lost and somehow her spirit is inside you.»

"Wha??? A girl? What girl? Some sort of ghoul? A ghost?"

«No, she's not dead yet, so she's not technically a ghost—I suppose you'd call her a spirit.»

"What the hell is she doing in *me*?"

«Well, we're not too sure about that ourselves, but these things happen sometimes. At any rate, we'd like to perform a kind of exorcism now, so if you could follow me, please.»

Follow you where?

They're all looking this way. Don't look at me, you assholes! Fuck you! Fuck—

Yoji.

Oh shit! That voice really *is* coming from inside my head. Some kind of evil spirit—this is fucking scary!

"What do you mean 'exorcism'?"

«I know it's a lot to ask, but if you could come with me to the clinic where the young woman is hospitalized, I'm sure we can clear the whole thing up in no time.»

Sounds like a lot of bullshit to me.

Hey, hold on just a minute.

"Are you telling me this girl inside my head is still alive?"

«She most certainly is.»

"So when you're done with this exorcism, she'll be a walking, talking normal girl?"

«I expect so.»

Hang on! That's a whole different ballgame. When did this girl get inside me? Can she finger me as the Round-and-Round Devil? I don't like the smell of this.

"No…no…I think I'm good just like this."

«Do you mean you're not going to give back the young lady's spirit?»

"Well, if she just popped inside me, she must be okay with that."

«It's not a matter of 'being okay'…»

Does this guy ever shut up?!

"I said I'm good, so fuck off!"

«Please don't get excited.»

"I'll show you excited—I'll bash your head in!"

Then chop you up and throw you in the river!

Huh?

What's happening? What's that on my back?

«What should we do? Tie him up and take him to the hospital?»

«That's a good idea, though it might not be so easy.»

 Ah, over there! A cop!

 "Officer, officer! Over here!"

«Please! Don't make such a fuss, especially on a solemn occasion like this.»

«Yes, please be quiet.»

"Let me go!"

«Relax, buddy. You're not going anywhere.»

"Do you know who you're dealing with?"

«Okay boys, hang on to him!»

"Get your hands off me!"

Got to get away!

"No! Let me go! Let me *go*!"

La di da di da di da. Shitbread, di di dum di dum.

Shitty di shit, his di dum gently embrace di dum di dum the shitbread. Di di di dum di dum. Di di li dum. I spy with my little eye a loverly prize buried deep in…*shit*! He he he he, ho ho ho ho, ha ha ha ha. A man's got to do what a man's got to…shit oh shit upon a shooting star…

That building over there should do…

And I've still got the four thousand in my pocket. I didn't give it to the Yoshibas after all. Who would have thought things would turn out like this? Life's funny that way. But I guess this is all I can expect. I'm free, and I can call my own shots.

The fire escape is down! Up we go!

I must be out of shape—feel all heavy.

La di da di da di dum di dum di shit, shit, shit, *shit*!

Some guy's coming after me, fast! He's going to catch me...got to...hurry!

Made it! The roof.

Over this *fence*!

No!

Uhhhhhh!

«Where do you think you're going? Give us back the girl!»

"I don't know what you're talking about! I don't know any girl!"

«Don't lie to me!»

"I'm telling the truth!"

I really *don't*! I have no idea what's going on!

I'll poke your fucking eyes out!

«Huh?»

"You asshole!"

Shitbread di dum di dum. The last time. For all the world's a shitbread, and we'll meet again, don't know where, don't know when...

Heh!

Chofu's a great big beautiful place!

Look at all those people down there. Try not to land on any of them.

Shit! I didn't think I would die before the old lady.

Yoji.

So, you're still here.

Would have liked to leave this world just a little better than I found it.

Wish I'd had time to finish my Asura Man, the little Buddha I was going to make out of those kids. That would have been a statue like the world has never seen!

Oh well. The Round-and-Round will now perform his patented quadruple somersault in the laid-out position…

Part Three:
Jump-Start My Heart

1

WHAT AM I? How did the monster inside me get plugged right into the Round-and-Round Devil? What's the link between the Round-and-Round and me?

The Round-and-Round is a different person, but somehow, metaphorically speaking, he's also *another* me. I'm a woman and he's a man, but that's the difference of just one sex chromosome. It doesn't amount to much. These days you've got men who like men and women who like women, people who feel like women living in men's bodies, and vice versa. You've got fairies and dykes and gays and homos and lesbians—and on top of that you've got half the people faking it. When it's all *that* confused, no one's going to care that the Round-and-Round's a man and I'm a woman. Come to think of it, it's not a bad analogy—you can't tell the difference between men and women anymore, just like the Round-and-Round and I can't tell who's who between the two of us, can't figure out where I leave off and he starts. It's almost like we're the same person—which may be more common than you think these days, now that we're all reading each other's thoughts online all the time. Kind of screws with the idea of the individual—one big group consciousness, like all those people on V of H following everything we do.

I guess you get all those creeps together inside one head and you actually *make* a monster.

And then there's the monster made out of pieces of all those kids in that dark forest inside me. Totally scary, stealing sounds and voices and doing all that evil shit. That was made by chopping up me and the Round-and-Round and a whole bunch of other kids and sticking us all together. I suppose it's still in there, chopping up more people and slapping them on to make itself even bigger. When you get so much bad karma together, something pretty monstrous happens. Like Armageddon.

So I guess that monster makes sense in a way, metaphorically speaking.

And even the Round-and-Round—he might be something that was already inside me.

I'm one single person, but I've got all of these different personalities and voices inside me. And that monster that took them and turned them all into those terrible songs…that was just me too. Which means—I'm just guessing here—that the way it looked, that awful crammed-together body, was somehow an image of something deep inside me, some fundamental core. Like my "ego" or something? Who knows? Or maybe it's more like… I'm somewhere deep inside myself in that dark forest and I'm sucking up all those people, all the ones inside of me, and cutting them up and incorporating them into myself, making them part of me and making myself bigger and bigger. Maybe that's it: I'm the monster. But I bet it's probably the same for everybody—we've all got a monster inside, in our own dark forest, grubbing up parts from a whole lot of other people.

That's probably it—we need to feed on others to make our inner monster grow. In the forest inside us, it's all-powerful, but what it wants is to be totally scary on the outside. And maybe the boundaries between those forests aren't always as clear as you think. Maybe some people have special powers that let them come and go from one to another whenever they want.

Tansetsu Sakurazuki. That pale, chubby, shaggy geek. Maybe he couldn't exactly come right into my forest, but once I was there, he managed to reach in and grab me. And all the weird stuff that happened to me on the way to the forest—all that must have been inside me as well. I mean, how likely is it that you'd escape from a hammer-swinging classmate and run into a bunch of TV celebrities, then get on the wrong train and end up being chased by the Mafia? All that must have been my imagination. But Tansetsu Sakurazuki came right in and collared me there by the cliff. Pretty cool. And if he can do it, then there must be other people who can too. And if people can get in and out of these inner-self places, that means there must be paths of some sort leading back and forth—even if not everybody has the power to use them. Paths between me and Tansetsu, between the Round-and-Round and me, between me and everybody else, between all of us.

Not that that makes me feel any better. The point here is that totally scary monster. I think it was probably just something inside me, but it might also be totally possible that it really exists somewhere. That out there in some real dark forest—not inside me or anybody else—a monster is really catching little kids, cutting them up in pieces, and sticking them onto its own body. If so, then maybe, while I was wandering around in limbo like that, I got called to that real dark forest, and those real kids—with names

I invented for them—helped me battle the monster.

Now *that's* a scary thought.

Then just suppose I really *was* eaten up by someone—someone I just decided to call "Olle"—whose face was on top of the monster's head, and that the monster really did swallow me. If you suppose all that, then maybe I'm still in the monster now. And I just haven't realized it yet since I'm still living in the world of phantasms.

But how can you tell? Am I still alive? Or did I die back there and it's just taking me a really long time to realize it? Am I just fooling around with all these illusions until I finish dying? I don't think I can tell the difference. I know I've been doing a lot of *really* crazy stuff, but have I *really* been doing it?—that's where I'm not so sure. I've been to all these totally *weird* places, and now it seems like I'm back where I started, one complete lap—but how do I *know* I'm back? Or not? And having Tansetsu Sakurazuki around isn't helping anything—he's so totally bizarre I don't know what he's going to do or where we're going to go. It wouldn't surprise me if he suddenly looked at his watch and said he was late, late for a very important date, and had to be going—but that he'd take me with him, anywhere I wanted to go, in exchange for a pair of my panties, and then giggle and take my hand and tap his heels together and we'd fly up into the sky. Wouldn't surprise me at all.

I suppose if that happened, I'd just have to cope. Maybe I'd end up someplace in the real world but still totally lost, or maybe we'd go to some other world. Who knows, I might even give him a pair of my panties, if I felt like it. It might be worth it just to see the look on his face.

But the one place I wouldn't want to go is back to that forest. I don't care whether it was real or a total fantasy. I don't ever want to be that scared again. If that's some sort of place you've got to pass through right before you die, then I may have to live forever.

So I guess for now I'm going to believe that the monster and the forest were things I made up inside me somewhere—that the world and I made up together. I don't much care whether the monster is just another me, or whether it's actually some sort of bridge between me and the Round-and-Round, or even a thread linking all of us together. As long as it's not really cutting up flesh-and-blood kids and mashing them together, it's all the same to me.

Though I guess if it's all just stuff I made up in my head, then there's a chance I'm not real either. "I think, therefore I am"—or something like that, but if I'm somehow stuck together with another person and we can go back and forth like that, then how do I know it's really "I" doing the "thinking"? I may *think* I'm "thinking," but it's possible that it's the other guy who's *really* thinking. You may think you're thinking all you want, but if it's someone else doing all that thinking, it doesn't add up to "I am." I guess.

So no one *really* knows whether they even exist or not—and they don't even realize they don't know. Because they haven't been through all this stuff that's been happening to me. But now I know. I have absolutely no idea what's real and what's made up, but at least I know that I don't know.

I know that the whole "I think therefore I am" thing is a pile of shit, but I also know there's nothing I can do about it. I can see that the "I am" part is pretty sketchy, but in the end that's fine by me. Shit, I'm pretty much fine with "I'm not." If anybody out there doubts my existence, I'm not putting up an argument.

And I'll tell you why: because all this stuff I've been doing, this whole life of mine—living with my brother, mooning over Yoji, fooling around with people other than Yoji for no good reason, the meaningless fights, dying, coming back—all of it has been a hell of a lot of fun. And that feeling—that *fun*—is absolutely real. I'm sure of it. So in the end, everything else is okay too. It's all okay. Not a problem. I even *enjoy* doubting my own existence. The ultimate purpose of life is to have fun. Even for people who don't think that's what they're aiming for, it still ends up coming first—always. People who are suffering end up *enjoying* the suffering, and people who are struggling *like* the struggle. Whatever it is you're doing now, you chose it on some level, and for you it's the most fun thing there is. So maybe that's why I totally rejected the monster and made the dark forest go away, because I really *don't* like fear and pain…which is why I'm here enjoying myself now—wherever here is.

It's great here.

Even though everything's still as stupid as it's always been.

2

In the north corner of Chofu, near the Nogawa River, there's a temple called Eiganji, and in that temple is an old statue of Asura, dark and gloomy, with the gold leaf peeling in places. The statue was supposedly carved by a man named Yoshitaka Koyama, though there's no way to know for sure. Anyway, this Yoshitaka Koyama was something of a known bad boy in these parts, and after doing something to totally piss off his parents, he ran away to the temple, and there, after various adventures, he saw the error of his ways and started carving images of the Buddha. At least that's how the story goes: bad boy mends his ways and takes up life as saintly artisan.

But I have a different theory. I think his interest in Buddha-carving actually came *before* he had this change of heart. It may have gone more like this: this Koyama is pretty much a creep of a guy...but even he can see that Buddha statues are beautiful... so why not try carving one?...and carving turns out to be *fun*... so why not take it up full time?...and a full-time Buddha-carver looks pretty much like a respectable guy...so now the creep looks respectable...and then it turns out it's actually *easier* to make your living respectably...so why not just *be* a respectable guy? At some point the question of whether you really are or aren't loses its meaning. Anyway, that's my theory about Koyama.

But then I actually went to Eiganji. Which I think was the first time I'd ever been to a temple. And I got to thinking about what it would be like to actually live there—in this really, really simple place where you do Zen, sitting all day *every* day, scrubbing the floors and reading sutras and all, and it occurred to me you might *really* turn into a stand-up guy in a place like that, might feel like you *had* to start carving Buddhas. I mean, human beings can't live without finding something enjoyable in life.

But for some reason, this Yoshitaka Koyama ended up making the same Asura over and over without ever being satisfied. He was apparently a real pro when it came to carving other Buddhas, popping them out like clockwork, but he could never finish the Asura. The head priest kept seeing his Asuras when they were almost finished, and he thought they were fantastic. He would even show up sometimes with collectors who wanted to buy them and were willing to pay top dollar, but Koyama would always say there was something wrong with the carving and immediately take an axe to it. The priest would be horrified, but he had no choice but to let him be. The rumor at the temple was that Koyama somehow saw some link between his former wicked self and the Asura statue, and since he was forever searching for a version of himself he could totally accept, he was forever remaking the statue. But I think that sort of misses the point. I think they were right that Koyama was identifying with the Asura, that he thought of it as somehow a double of himself, but I don't think he kept making it over because he was looking for some perfect version. I think Koyama found his own special bliss in the act of *destroying* the Asura. In other words, since the Asura was him, by chopping it to bits again and again and again, he was actually obliterating himself.

I'd go further than that. I think that deep down most people would be tempted to destroy themselves—as long as it didn't involve any real, bullet-to-the-brain kind of pain. We're not all totally in love with ourselves—not by a mile. And for those of us who aren't, for the ones who don't really like themselves much at all, destroying the self can look like a pretty decent option, especially if it comes with the chance of a fresh start. Lots of people feel there's something missing in the self they got dealt, something incomplete, unripe. So what's the point of struggling on with it? These folks opt for destroying the old, unsatisfactory self in favor of a new one. Basically, they just hit the reset button on life. And what about that wouldn't be great? Totally awesome. I suppose most of us feel that way, at least a little bit, some of the time. I know I do. For instance, when I was there by the cliff, and Yoji told me he didn't really feel "that way" about me, what did I do? I let go of Tansetsu's hand—because I felt for a minute that I wanted to die. Something inside me was tempted by the idea of being reborn as someone else, moving on in the great circle of transmigrating souls. If I could have looked back at myself just then, I would have probably wanted to take an axe to that failed monster called "me."

On the other hand, how do you know the new you is going

to be any better? You don't, of course. Anyway, to get back to the point: the Asura statue.

Koyama saw himself in the Asura because Asura himself had been something of a bad boy at the beginning. I don't know the details, but apparently before he became a god he went around making trouble for the Buddha and generally acting out. But clearly something happened; he underwent some sort of conversion under the Buddha's influence, and he became a good god himself.

Never underestimate the Buddha.

I know I don't. Though I have to admit I've got my own personal image of Him, my own personal-version God—put together just the way I like Him.

My God doesn't punish people like the Christian god, or scold them or test them. He just waits, with infinite compassion, for people to achieve enlightenment. He's never impatient. Time doesn't matter one bit to my God. Those impatient gods tend to make up trials and tribulations and punish you if you don't get them right, but my God is easygoing and optimistic, so He's willing to wait, with those narrow, smiley eyes of His, until you have a change of heart. Just wait and wait. He knows that if He waits long enough, any bad boy—or bad *god*, for that matter— will eventually see the light and stop doing all that bad stuff. Just like you eventually get tired of playing the same character all the time in a computer game, you eventually get tired of being bad; and when you're really tired of it, when you're fed up with it completely, you might end up doing something just a little bit good. And doing something even a little bit good means you must have some good in you, and people who have some good in them are basically good people. Or good gods. From there, even though they may have had just a tiny little taste of the doing-good-life, it's a sure bet these newly good people, or gods, when confronted with the *totally amazing, totally infinite* compassion of my God, will *totally* figure out that it's actually easier to live as a good guy.

Which is what must have happened with Asura, more or less. Maybe. I don't really know. But let's say it did anyway. I prefer to think it did.

So to continue this line of reasoning: Hideo Ozaki, the Round-and-Round Devil, killed those three Yoshiba boys—Shin'ichi, Koji, and Yuzo—and cut them up to try to make a statue of Asura. Though the truth is nobody really knows whether he killed them *because* he wanted to make an Asura or whether the idea of making the statue occurred to him only *after* he'd killed them. Three heads and six arms—Koyama's Asura had the same extra parts. So were Hideo Ozaki and Yoshitaka Koyama feeling the same kinds of feelings when they set out to make their statues?

In a basic sense, they were—or at least something pretty similar. Ozaki even started calling the statue he wanted to make "Asura Man." Which is why, in the moment before he died, after he had jumped from the roof of that apartment house, in the instant it took him to fall seven stories, there was absolutely no trace of regret or remorse in his heart—which I know for a fact because we were linked together—and that was because he believed that by trying to make his Asura statue, he had hoped to leave the world a slightly better place. He was convinced his "Asura Man" would have been the real deal—not just a toy superman but the image of God.

At this point, of course, I can't help thinking about that monster—the one I met in the heart of the forest. He had a lot of faces and arms too. Wasn't he just another—totally gross—Asura?

But if so, then I guess I was doing just what the Round-and-Round was doing: cutting up those kids to make my own god—and mine was even bigger than his, with more kids and more parts. I do feel pretty bad for those kids, if they're still there in the forest. But it might make them feel a little better to know that the Round-and-Round was working with totally dead boys. My kids were suffering a lot, but at least they were still alive…Well *thanks*, Aiko!

I guess you're right: the difference doesn't amount to much.

Anyway, you still have to admit that Hideo Ozaki's basic idea— to make a statue of Asura—was a good one, a good impulse… and the fact that he was trying to do something good means that Ozaki himself had some good in him, even if it was just a little tiny bit. And a person who has some good in him can be said to be a good person, at least in some limited way. So in some limited way, Ozaki was a good person. Even if he was the Round-and-Round Devil.

So I would like to follow the example of my own made-up God and exercise great patience and totally awesome compassion… and forgive the Round-and-Round Devil. I would like to say that I even love him.

And I'd like to do the same for myself—forgive me, love me. Regardless of how stupid and selfish I've been, how much I've insisted on wasting this precious life, I've still got a few good points…though I can't think of any at the moment. Still, I'm sure I have some—at least one or two. Somewhere. Probably.

But let's forget about me.

Hideo Ozaki, the Round-and-Round Devil. Pushing thirty, unemployed, living with his parents, spoiled, abusive, hanging out, following V of H—and all the while building up this tremendous stress, this awful pressure. He starts looking around for a way to vent his anger and frustration, and what he sees is the terrible stuff these middle school kids have been doing, these little monstrous kid-killers—Sakakibara and the rest of them. So, half as a joke, he kills a few cats, then a few dogs, and I think you can safely say that it's just a short step to killing the three boys. Hideo Ozaki, the Round-and-Round Devil…just another bad-boy Asura.

So despite his really, really bad choice of materials, you *might* say that Ozaki himself *became* a good Asura when he set out to make one…though you'd be *totally* lying if you did. But maybe you could at least say that he was taking the very first little baby steps on the road to Asura-hood, or maybe that he had at least discovered there *was* such a road…or maybe that he'd noticed some vague signs that might have eventually led him to discovering that there was such a road…Anyway, for me anyway, the fact that he wanted to make an Asura is at the very least a sign there was some good somewhere in his heart…

So, though I did hesitate for a while, in the end I told Sayaka Yoshiba why I thought her three boys had been cut to pieces. I told her that Shin'ichi, Koji, and Yuzo had become an Asura.

Now of course I knew this wasn't going to solve her problem. I knew she wasn't going to thank me for explaining and tell me it was all right now. No, I knew it was only going to make her even crazier with grief and anger. And I wondered why I'd been brought back to this world if that was the best news I'd learned on the other side. But I also knew that time can heal anything—well, most things anyway—and I had my hopes that the photos of the Koyama Asura that the investigators found in Hideo Ozaki's apartment might actually help in the long run. He had taken hundreds of them—beautiful, pure pictures of the statue—and part of me hoped that someday, if only in a small, provisional way, they might give just a little comfort to Mrs. Yoshiba's suffering soul.

The death of her children remained completely incomprehensible—nothing would ever change that—but maybe there was some peace to be had in figuring out one small part of the puzzle.

Eiganji was not far from the Yoshiba home, and Sayaka started going there almost every day. She would sit in front of the image of Asura and stare at it for a long time. At first she just wept bitterly, sometimes talking to it or even screaming. But as the days passed she seemed to grow calmer, the tears less frequent.

Yoji Kaneda was usually there too.

On the night of the Armageddon, as he was heading back to the station from my house, Yoji had found Mrs. Yoshiba, still on that bench in the park. Her husband had left her and gone home, and she was just sitting there, staring off into space. He had tried to talk to her, and then he had taken her home, but when they got there they found that her husband was already dead. I guess all hell broke loose at that point, but that was also the moment Yoji got my frantic, selfish phone call. So he had run out, right in the middle of Armageddon and the confusion at the Yoshibas', to come back to my house—and there he had found me, more or less half dead, my head split open by Maki Saito's hammer. Poor Yoji—too many surprises!

So he'd taken me to the hospital and stayed with me until I was in intensive care. I was in pretty bad shape, but I guess he knew he couldn't really do anything more for me, so he decided to go where he could do some good: back to a mother who had lost her three children…and now her husband. She would need help with the wake and the funeral, and so he had gone back to her—which is how Sayaka Yoshiba took Yoji away from me.

Sometimes I show up at Eiganji too, along with Tansetsu Sakurazuki. He usually brings a bag packed with cups and two thermoses of tea—one has hot *hojicha* and the other, cold green tea. He roasts the hojicha himself, and the green tea is some special blend. They're both pretty tasty. And he makes these awesome

cakes too. Today, it was bean dumplings—soft little mochi filled
with yummy bean jam. Jam *and* mochi both homemade. I told him
that if fortune-telling doesn't pan out, he could always open a sweet
shop. But he said he was doing just fine, thank you very much.

You go through the gate at Eiganji and straight ahead until you
reach the main hall. Inside, just to the right of the big Buddha, is
Yoshitaka Koyama's Asura. There, in front of it, on cushions set
on top of these thin grass mats, which are themselves spread right
on the cold earth floor, are Sayaka Yoshiba and my idiot friend
Yoji. You can tell right away that the bond between them is really
powerful—even if it's not very old—and I have to admit that's
pretty hard for me to take. I mean I *am* still recovering from being
half dead—and having a broken heart. So seeing them together
makes me kind of queasy. Though I know there's nothing to be
done about it. I'm hardly the first girl to have loved and lost.

And I guess the truth is, these days, I'm pretty far from being
"pretty fucking far from okay." If that's not too complicated. What
I mean is, my troubles now don't compare to the ones the girls had
in *Caged Fury*.

You can't give up and die over a little thing like being dumped
by Yoji. You know that now, Aiko.

When Tansetsu and I show up at Eiganji, Mrs. Yoshiba smiles
and gets up to greet us. She's so calm and gentle that you could
never imagine she's the same woman I'd seen crying her eyes out
and fucking her husband's brains out on that park bench. She's
totally beautiful too. Scary beautiful.

Oh well.

That's just the way it is. I don't have to like it, but that doesn't
change anything. So be it.

Yoji takes a breath and gets right up with Sayaka—which
makes me want to actually puke.

Remain calm, Aiko.

Cicadas are crying in the trees around the temple. Tansetsu gives us each a cup and pours the hojicha. It hurts my throat to drink hot tea on a hot day, but then he pours the green tea, and I realize the contrast makes the cool tea taste unbelievably delicious. I also realize we've still got the mochi cakes. They're slightly sweet and have this amazing spongy texture. I could eat the whole plate of them, but Tansetsu gives us just one each. Maybe he thinks good things come in small packages, or small servings, or something like that. But they are *sooooo* delicious, I wish he'd let me have more! I'm still a growing girl. But it's one-to-a-customer, so I might as well give up. I'll ask for more tea instead.

When we're done with our snack, I realize that the Buddha and the Asura and the shadows haven't calmed me down much—in fact, the vibes I'm getting from Yoji and Mrs. Yoshiba have had just the opposite effect. So I decide to go for a walk around the temple. Tansetsu gathers up his teacups and thermoses and follows me out of the hall.

We head for the cemetery. There are long rows of tombs with just a few trees planted between them, and the sun is intense. Afraid I might get sunburned, I try to hide in Tansetsu's shadow. I think I'm being pretty subtle about it, but he probably knows what I'm up to—he's a mind-reader, after all. It seems he recently started studying to be a weather forecaster as well, and now he's telling me all about the wind and the clouds and the air pressure. Usually, nothing could bore me more, but I end up listening in spite of myself. He's so intense when he gets going about this stuff that I almost find it interesting. There must be *something* to it if he can keep yakking on forever like that. But finally I decide I was right in the first place: there's not much interesting about wind and clouds and air pressure. Nothing at all, in fact. But far more interesting than *what* he's saying, for me, is the *way* he says it—the way he tucks his hair behind his ears…just like that teacher on TV, Kinpachi or whatever he was called. In fact, everything about him reminds me of some goofy TV character—except Tansetsu is even funnier! I realize it's been a long time since I've laughed the way he makes me laugh.

"How's work going?" I ask. I know he's older than me—ten years older, in fact—but somehow I want to sound like we're equals. Plus, he doesn't look his age—nothing like it. I wonder how old he *does* look, and then I realize he doesn't look *any* age in particular. There's really no way to tell.

By "work" I mean the jobs he gets using his psychic powers to contact dead people. Sayaka had hired him because she really wanted to talk to her boys.

But when I bring up his "work," he frowns.

He hadn't had any luck contacting the little boys, he explains. They were hardly old enough to talk when they died, so when he tried calling them from this side, they probably didn't understand—or maybe they were too little to even go to the place where other dead people go. He was still looking for a way to reach them.

He didn't mention it, but I knew he might also be having a cash-flow problem. He had pretty much given up his fortune-telling business for the time being while he was working for Mrs. Yoshiba, and he wouldn't be paid until he got results. It occurred to me that Sano's family would probably have been willing to pay him for finding Sano's body, but I decided not to mention it.

Then, out of the blue—and I'm not sure why—I asked if he had a girlfriend, and he got this creepy grin on his face. "No," he said, "but I'm open to suggestions." So I cut things off right there.

Am I ever going to find the right boyfriend? A truly fine boyfriend?

I remember those cliffs. The second time around, after I got away from the Round-and-Round and was swimming upstream in the River Styx with all those other souls, ready to go over to the other side. But then up there, written in solid rock on the world-of-the-living-side cliff, was a message for me.

Aiko!
Come back!

I decided to ignore it and go on, but then I heard this really loud voice.

"Hey! Aiko!"

And I looked up and there was that weird, age-free Tansetsu Sakurazuki, waving to me from the top of the cliff. Grinning for all he was worth. As though he was really, really happy to see me. And it was the kindness in that smile that brought me back to this side. Or sometimes I think about the first time I was there, between life and death, the way he reached out and grabbed my collar—the look on his face, the feel of his hand. In fact, I think about it a lot. All the time, in fact.

He had this really firm grip, but there was something reassuring about it at the same time. And his face had a lot of "character"—a little weird, but in a nice way.

Shit, shit, shit!

Now part of me was even thinking it might be nice to *do* it with this totally weird guy. But the thing is—I like them *cute*. Or at least somewhat normal looking…like Yoji. Yoji!

And I've given that up, haven't I? Never again will I do it with somebody I don't like. Didn't I promise myself that?

The next time it's going to be with someone I'm crazy about. Someone who's crazy about me, who'll treat me right and take care of me. Someone who'd fight tooth and nail to protect me. Someone I care about, someone I love more than anyone else, someone *I'd* fight tooth and nail to protect. Somebody who'd stop my heart with one look—and who would then come running to jump-start it again!

If I could find somebody like that, it would be love at first sight. I'd fall totally in love with every inch of him. Not some part of him, or something about him, or in some certain way, but in every way, with every bit of him, the very core, the very essence of him. My heart's jump-starter would have the kind of face that would pop into my head the minute I started thinking about love…

Hold on a second.

What is Tansetsu's face doing popping into my head? Must be some kind of mistake. Maybe I just feel grateful to him for bringing me back from the land of the dead—maybe that's why I spend so much time thinking about his geeky face. And it is *totally* geeky—the long, straight hair down over the ears, that dopey look—but maybe the popping is natural enough if you factor in the minor detail that he saved my life.

It couldn't be love, could it?

And then there was still Sano.

He's probably still out there, dead somewhere. I finally mentioned him to Tansetsu, and he got in touch with Sano's family. They hired him to try to find the body. Hmm. I guess when I think about it now, I realize that Sano was probably a little bit in love with me. Maybe that's why he was calling to me from the other side. And maybe everybody kept telling me I should sleep with him because they knew how he felt about me. Maybe Kan...well, who knows?

Anyway, if you really were in love with me, then I'm sorry. Forgive me, Sano. But I really didn't like you. And don't call me anymore. Don't come around inviting me to join you on the other side. I've decided I'm going to go on living here in this world, just as I am, and I'll find someone other than you...someone I really *like* doing it with.

Though I have no idea who it's going to be.

So I think I'll tell Tansetsu not to look for you. I guess you still kind of give me the creeps.

Still, it's pretty incredible to think that you could love somebody so much you'd call to them from beyond death, try to get them to join you on the other side. But if you ask me, it would have made more sense for him to try to get me to bring him back to the land of the living, to jump-start his heart.

"What?"

Early summer. I'm walking with Tansetsu on the jogging path by the Nogawa River, thinking about everything and nothing, glancing over at him from time to time, when I suddenly realize he's been talking to me.

"You know, Aiko," he had said, "you really should read more, and not just crappy manga. Books broaden your horizons. And TV and movies too. Try something new, learn about the world. You should start reading the newspaper, stop spending so much time on those worthless websites. Get out and have fun, meet new people."

"I'm not sure what you're getting at," I said.

"What I'm trying to say is...I was there at the river, in your inner world, and I saw all that stuff in your imagination—and I hate to say it, but I wasn't too impressed. It's a reflection of everything you've seen and done—your whole life—and from what I saw, I'd say you could use a little inner-life enrichment."

Remind me to kill him someday.

And when he's dead and going off to cross his own River Styx, remind me *not* to save him. Though I suppose you have to have psychic powers like his to write on those cliffs anyway.

The Nogawa is really narrow, and it has all these short little bridges going across. As we get close to the next one, I seriously consider turning and crossing to the other side to show him how pissed off I am…but then I don't. For now anyway, this side I'm on with Tansetsu is the right side.

Otaro Maijo (1973-) is a novelist from Fukui, where most of his stories take place. Most of the illustrations in his novels were drawn by himself. He debuted with his mystery novel, *Kemuri ka tsuchi ka kuimono* (Smoke, Soil, or Food), with which he won the Mephisto Prize. He started writing pure literature with *Kuma no basho* (Place of the Bear), which was nominated for the Mishima Yukio Prize. Then in 2003, he won the Mishima Yukio Prize for *Asura Girl*.

THE
BATTLE ROYALE
BR
SLAM BOOK

EDITED BY HAIKASORU

KOUSHUN TAKAMI'S *BATTLE ROYALE* IS AN INTERNATIONAL
BEST SELLER, THE BASIS OF THE CULT FILM, AND
THE INSPIRATION FOR A POPULAR MANGA. AND FIFTEEN
YEARS AFTER ITS INITIAL RELEASE, *BATTLE ROYALE*
REMAINS A CONTROVERSIAL POP CULTURE PHENOMENON.

JOIN *NEW YORK TIMES* BEST-SELLING AUTHOR JOHN SKIPP,
BATMAN SCREENWRITER SAM HAMM, PHILIP K.DICK
AWARD-NOMINATED NOVELIST TOH ENJOE, AND AN ARRAY
OF WRITERS, SCHOLARS, AND FANS IN DISCUSSING GIRL
POWER, FIREPOWER, PROFESSIONAL WRESTLING, BAD
MOVIES, THE SURVIVAL CHANCES OF HOLLYWOOD'S LEADING
TEEN ICONS IN A BATTLE ROYALE, AND SO MUCH MORE!

$14.99 USA // $16.99 CAN // £9.99 UK   ISBN: 978-1-4215-6599-6

BATTLE ROYALE
— R E M A S T E R E D —

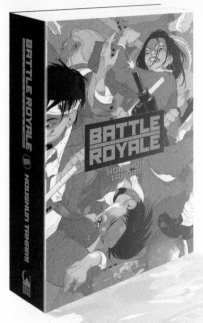

Koushun Takami's notorious high-octane thriller is based on an irresistible premise: a class of junior high school students is taken to a deserted island where, as part of a ruthless authoritarian program, they are provided arms and forced to kill one another until only one survivor is left standing.

Criticized as violent exploitation when first published in Japan—where it then proceeded to become a runaway best seller—*Battle Royale* is a *Lord of the Flies* for the 21st century, a potent allegory of what it means to be young and (barely) alive in a dog-eat-dog world. Made into a controversial hit movie of the same name, *Battle Royale* is already a contemporary Japanese pulp classic, now available in a new English-language translation.

$16.99 USA // $19.99 CAN // £9.99 UK   ISBN: 978-1-4215-6598-9

BATTLE ROYALE

ANGELS' BORDER

STORY BY KOUSHUN TAKAMI // ART BY MIOKO OHNISHI & YOUHEI OGUMA

A *BATTLE ROYALE* MANGA

FINALLY, DISCOVER THE POIGNANT, TRAGIC STORY OF THE GIRLS IN THE LIGHTHOUSE.

HARUKA TANIZAWA IS AN AVERAGE JUNIOR HIGH STUDENT. SHE PLAYS ON THE VOLLEYBALL TEAM AND JUST FELL IN LOVE FOR THE FIRST TIME. BUT HER LOVE IS ALSO HER BEST FRIEND AND CLASSMATE, YUKIE, AND HARUKA DREADS THE TRUTH COMING OUT AND RUINING THEIR RELATIONSHIP.

AND THEN HER ENTIRE CLASS IS DRUGGED, DRAGGED TO A DESERTED ISLAND AND FORCED TO PARTICIPATE IN THE BLOODY SPECTACLE OF THE PROGRAM.

WHILE MOST OF THE STUDENTS SCATTER AS SOON AS THEY'RE RELEASED FROM THE STAGING GROUNDS, YUKIE COMES BACK FOR HARUKA, AND TOGETHER THEY GATHER SOME OF THE OTHER GIRLS IN THE DUBIOUS SAFETY OF THE ISLAND'S LIGHTHOUSE.

THEY KNOW SURVIVAL IS UNLIKELY.
BUT WHAT ABOUT HOPE...?

$12.99 USA // $14.99 CAN // £8.99 UK | 5.75"x8.25" | ISBN: 978-1-4215-7168-3

HAIKASORU
THE FUTURE IS JAPANESE

PHANTASM JAPAN
—EDITED BY HAIKASORU

The secret history of the most famous secret agent in the world. A bunny costume that reveals the truth in our souls. The unsettling notion that Japan itself may be a dream. The tastiest meal you'll never have, a fedora-wearing neckbeard's deadly date with a yokai, and the worst work shift anyone—human or not—has ever lived through. Welcome to *Phantasm Japan*.

EDGE OF TOMORROW (MOVIE TIE-IN EDITION)
—HIROSHI SAKURAZAKA

When the alien Mimics invade, Keiji Kiriya is just one of many recruits shoved into a suit of battle armor called a Jacket and sent out to kill. Keiji dies on the battlefield, only to be reborn each morning to fight and die again and again. On his 158th iteration, he gets a message from a mysterious ally—the female soldier known as the Full Metal Bitch. Is she the key to Keiji's escape or his final death? Now a major motion picture starring Tom Cruise and Emily Blunt!

APPARITIONS: GHOSTS OF OLD EDO
—MIYUKI MIYABE

In old Edo, the past was never forgotten. It lived alongside the present in dark corners and in the shadows. In these tales, award-winning author Miyuki Miyabe explores the ghosts of early modern Japan and the spaces of the living world—workplaces, families, and the human soul—that they inhabit. Written with a journalistic eye and a fantasist's heart, *Apparitions* brings the restless dead, and those who encounter them, to life.